A Look To The Future Through The Eyes of an Eighty Year Old Pirate

Bowen Craig

In association with Bilbo Books

iUniverse, Inc.
Bloomington

iUniverse books may be ordered through booksellers or by contacting:

iUniverse
1663 Liberty Drive
Bloomington, IN 47403
www.iuniverse.com
1-800-Authors (1-800-288-4677)

ISBN: 978-1-4502-8619-0 (sc)
ISBN: 978-1-4502-8620-6 (ebk)

Printed in the United States of America

iUniverse rev. date: 10/29/2012

I'm dedicating this book to my mother, the
Super 7 and Mr. Jimmy Buffet.

The title, *A Look To The Future Through The Eyes Of An Eighty Year Old Pirate*, is taken from one of the classic works of art of our time, *Wacky Bananas*, authored by the great Walker Hubbs.

So, there's this dingy little dive bar in my town. I used to go there when I wanted to hide from the world. It's one of those isolated places that has so few patrons that it makes you wonder how it's able to stay in business, but it does have one regular.

He was a crusty old guy, a raging drunk and a fascinating storyteller.

He's one of those guys who long ago basically divorced himself from most of what we call "life", making him a great observer. I used to pull up a stool next to him, buy him rounds and listen. This aging pirate used to tell me about the strange, wonderful and horrific details of the nut-job age in which we live. Sometimes he'd tell a little story. Sometimes he'd just describe people he knew. Other times he'd just rant or joke. Toward the end of the night, his stories usually took a turn for the raunchy. And then he'd feel guilty and talk about his mother.

He might not have always told the literal truth, but he still managed to say what he wanted.

Table of Contents

CULT OF STEVE

In retrospect, it was bound to happen. History had proven it time and time again: Power-mad totalitarian leaders, attractive pop icons, Lee Iacocca. It's fact. If your face is plastered up all over the place, people will worship you and you'll start to believe that you're actually worthy of being worshipped.

Steve Meachem had sort of fallen into his job. He hadn't dreamt glory-fueled childhood dreams of being an insurance salesman. Who does? He hadn't been preparing for his job since toddlerhood, selling anti-bullying policies on the playground. He barely had even known what insurance was until he started selling it to people. But, it turned out that Steve Meachem was a damn good insurance salesman.

Steve had a broad, welcoming smile, a 1940s superhero chin dimple, wide cheekbones, nice business-brown hair, and big trustworthy blue eyes. He had the standard salesmen accessories too: a perky wife who volunteered with the right organizations, two gorgeous kids who fit perfectly on a holiday card, the right car of the moment, nice suits, even a happy black and white labradoodle.

Yes, Steve's life was going well. He was making money. His family life was to be admired and envied. His trivia team was second in the region. And then they put his face up on that billboard.

There's a reason that insurance agents need people to see their giant faces floating above them, and it's a pretty simple plan—amazing in its simplicity. It's God-like. That's it. And who could better provide you with money after a flood than God?

Steve didn't demand that people sacrifice animals to him at first. That came later. He didn't purposefully start wearing long flowing robes and change his employees' uniforms to add a billy club holster to ensure that no one looks him directly in the eye. He didn't immediately start only using human furniture.

At first Steve just made some rather strange pronouncements to his secretaries:

"Let every third customer receive these wafers and get discounted renters insurance."

"I declare that we shall no longer sell earthquake insurance to people named Marge."

"Bring me two virgins and a falafel."

The staff was a little perplexed, but Steve was a good boss, so they went along with it.

But as time went on, Steve was growing progressively more God-like in his pronouncements. That second floating head of Steve billboard didn't help.

He began to mandate that all of his clients spend at least an hour a day kneeling in front of one of his billboards. People trust insurance agents. People trust Steve. So, they did as he commanded.

Steve's wife was a little miffed when, in the middle of a garden club meeting, he claimed two of his neighbors' wives as his own. His nephew did raise an objection when, on his wedding night, Steve cited the right of *Prima Nocta*. And prospective insurance buyers were a little confused when he would, often, from the seat of his human throne, command them to dance and juggle for his amusement before they could buy car insurance. But it's the law. You've got to have car insurance and Steve's was the only floating head in town.

Steve Meachem might just have gone down in Comment, Georgia lore as a strange, conceited insurance agent if they hadn't put up that third billboard. Comment is a small town, and, so you could, by that point, pretty much see Steve's smiling face from anywhere inside the city limits. This did not have a positive effect on Steve.

He rewrote his will so that not only will he be buried with a working telephone (in case God calls), but his secretaries are to be buried alive with him.

"Let there be only one form of insurance in this town—Wrath of Steve Insurance—it shall be a full service policy."

"Let not my seed touch the ground."

"The month of June shall henceforth be known as Steve."

The national insurance group to which Steve belonged would've protested about some of Steve's more obscure changes, but the man could flat out sell insurance, and insurance agencies aren't exactly known for their humanity, so they let it slide. They made fun of him behind his back at the national conference in Vegas, sure, but otherwise they let him be.

Still, they never should've put up that fourth billboard. That was the straw that broke the camel's back.

After that, Steve's pronouncements went a little too far. His decree that his secretaries build a giant flat billboard to span four counties so that his face could be seen from space was basically a non-starter. Although the city council did allow him to rename the local high school sports' team mascot The Fighting Steves, Steve had no power outside of the city limits.

Steve's idea that all Halloween costumes be him also didn't work. Kids rarely want to dress up like insurance agents. His own kids went along with it, but only after he threatened to smite them.

Steve's petition to the state to allow his agency to stop paying property taxes, ala churches, didn't fly in the Atlanta halls of government, under the dome. When he demanded that the local radio station only play songs about him, that also didn't go over well (mainly because there weren't that many songs about Steve . . . yet). And that was probably the thing that caused the state to begin its investigation.

Of course, Steve's agency was shut down. People still bought insurance, but not from Steve. And the good people of Comment, Georgia breathed a collective sigh of relief when they saw new agent Bobby Tomlinson's face hoisted up onto that first billboard. The city council quickly voted to limit the number of giant insurance agent face billboards in town to one per salesman.

AMERICAN ROYALTY

It goes without saying of course, but Dirk Peters was the most famous man in the world. As a prodigious child, Dirk played the role of Little Jimmy Smiley, the wisecracking, but terminally cute, scamp on the hit TV series, *The Black Family Adopts White Kids*. America fell in love with Dirk and every time Dirk was in public, the adoring throngs of fans would shout his catchphrase, "Ooopsy Doopsy" at him, as if he didn't have to say that line four thousand times a year. They say that's the price of fame.

Many child stars burn out faster than you can say Todd Bridges, but not Dirk. Playing a street-wise teenage junkie turned social worker with magical powers in the film *Written By Studio Executives*, solidified Dirk's place in our hearts. When he woke up and saw that needle still in his arm, Dirk's character, Bubbles McQueen, decided to turn his life around, just like all of those women on Lifetime. And we loved him for it.

Changing directions, Dirk wrote, directed and starred in his own one-man show. It was called *Stripped Down* and Dirk cleverly revealed a few minor Hollywood secrets and his own struggles with Albuterol and throat lozenges while simultaneously taking off his clothes and showing off his killer abs, to the delight of young women everywhere.

His next film role was to be his most challenging part yet. Dirk played a wounded Army veteran turned head in a jar kept alive by being attached to the robot body of David Hasselhoff. The critics all agreed that while viewing the film was scientifically proven to make you lose brain cells, Dirk did a hell of a job. He won the Academy Award for Best Portrayal of An Ugly Person by a Good Looking Person, narrowly beating out Matt Damon who played the lead in The Ben Affleck Story.

Now Dirk was an international phenomenon. He was one of those Hollywood actors who now had the overpoweringly naïve confidence to believe that his good looks and catchy sound bites could save the world.

It's a fairly common disease in Southern California known medically as Barbara Streisyndrome.

So, naturally, Dirk signed up with an international humanitarian relief organization and was sent overseas to stop wars. His first stop was Tibet, the cause celebre' of naïve hippies who think a bumper sticker on a Geo in Vermont is going to affect Chinese domestic policy. After Dirk had talked to the Chinese government and the Tibetan people, he left, feeling confident that his winning smile and sexy butt would solve the problem, but he'd failed to take into account cultural differences, like the Chinese habit of not giving a shit what teenagers think.

Dirk's next stop was the Middle East. He felt that, although politicians, religious leaders, good Samaritans, and the United Nations had so far failed to bridge the Israeli/Palestinian gap, very few Hollywood actors had even tried. Attracting a crowd in the West Bank, Dirk announced for all to hear:

"Look people, I know you two groups have been killing each other for a while and I realize that you have religious differences and revenge pacts, but I'm good looking, like really good looking, so let's just stop all this violence."

Dirk felt more accomplished than he had since that time he'd found that homeless guy behind his house and had generously let the man stare at him for two hours while he did push-ups. Dirk's next destination was Africa, where he would be torn limb from limb for trying to settle the eons-old feud between hippopotami and water buffalo.

Dirk Peters was a man who tried to change the world. He failed, but you have to admit that he was really good looking

POLITICS IS REGRESSIVE

Conservatives are like fourteen year old boys. Liberals are like toddlers. Think about it.

Conservatives and fourteen year old boys think about sex all the time, but never get any.

Liberals and toddlers both cry and whine . . . a lot.

Conservatives and fourteen year old boys both think they can eat anything and never get fat.

Liberals and toddlers both rely on handouts and sleep a good portion of the day.

Conservatives and fourteen year old boys both have to sneak around to have any fun . . . and then lie about it.

Liberals and toddlers both like breasts.

Conservatives and fourteen year old boys both have unwavering beliefs in things that have been proven untrue time and again, like trickle down economics and that they'll wind up different than their parents.

Liberals and toddlers both need to be held when it rains and told that everything's gonna be all right.

Conservatives and fourteen year old boys both don't want to learn anything new.

Liberals and toddlers both prefer to be up all night, screaming.

Conservatives and fourteen year old boys both swallow whatever crap is fed to them.

Liberals and toddlers both don't work.

Conservatives and fourteen year old boys both hang around people who think exactly like they do and make fun of anyone who thinks differently.

Liberals and toddlers both can babble endlessly about stuff that nobody understands or cares about.

YET ANOTHER GRAND HOAX FOISTED ON US ALL

You probably thought that the great Milli Vanilli fiasco was the first time that the recording industry tried to pull a fast one on us and replace the singer/songwriter with a better-suited cover man or men. You don't even know how wrong you were. I do. You were really wrong. Really, really wrong. You're a stupid, stupid, idiot who believes whatever people tell you. You might want to consider suicide. But I digress.

The first big musical hoax of recent times was, in fact, much bigger and widespread than a pop group who could kind of dance, but not even kind of sing, in the late 1980s. The, arguably, most popular musician in modern times was a fake. I'm talking about Bob Marley.

Bob Marley wasn't a peaceful, pot-loving, hippie, Rastafarian, Jamaican guy who inspired the world. He was an out-of-work, redneck, refrigerator repairman from just outside of Natchez, Mississippi. Of course, nobody knows this since the music industry did such a great job of covering it all up and twisting his meaning to give purpose, love, and hope to teenagers and people who believe Ralph Nader.

It took me a while to realize the truth, but I figured it out one day in line at the Dairy Queen when I met the real Bob Marley. He was buying a Blizzard for his infant daughter and we bonded over a shared love of jimmies. So, over a meal where I watched him destroy his child's metabolism for life, he told me the whole story. He told me how a music industry executive named Arno O'Rourke, had taken Bob's tunes and turned them into something else, twisted their original meanings. And, after 45 minutes I came to the inescapable conclusion that the music industry was right to do what they did. This guy was a sadistic weirdo.

Apparently, the music honchos twisted the original meanings of all of redneck Bob's songs to something shall we say more hopeful.

NO WOMAN NO CRY—It's actually an ode to domestic violence. Bob was beating the crap out of his wife one day when inspiration struck.

THREE LITTLE BIRDS—He composed it while in his deer stand. Originally, their message to you-oo-oo was "make it a kill shot".

BUFFALO SOLDIER—This is what he called himself after, on a trip to Minnesota, he had anal sex with a bison.

GET UP, STAND UP—Bob Marley liked to taunt people in wheelchairs.

JAMMIN—Originally this was an ode to deflowering underage girls. They did keep the line, "I hope you like jamming too".

I SHOT THE SHERRIFF—Yeah, they pretty much kept this one it tact, but they cut the rest of the chorus—it was originally, "I Shot the Sheriff, and then Tied the Deputy Down to an Anthill after Covering him with Honey and Peeing on Him".

EXODUS—It was supposed to be a song about being banned from Epcot for attempting to have marital relations with Goofy.

So, as you can see, sometimes music executives do get it right. Sometimes the lie is better than the truth. Sometimes it's preferable to sing those songs of freedom without knowing that what Bob really wanted to be redeemed for was shoving one too many squirrels into yet another medical cadaver's anus.

THE REAL REASON THAT WE STOPPED LETTING DOGS VOTE

I'm one of the only ones left who can remember. I'm one of the only ones left who even *wants* to remember. Nobody believes me when I tell them, but it's true. Dogs used to vote. They were a legitimate and powerful part of the country's electorate . . . too powerful. Of course they whitewashed the history books and people forget, as always. But I won't forget. I won't *ever* forget.

America was young, free, in love. It was a grand experiment. The Bill of Rights was the first time that a government had ever codified and enshrined into law the rights of its citizens. But history has conveniently forgotten about the tenth and a half Amendment—'Being necessary for a free society, the rights of canines to cast votes shall not be abridged'. In retrospect, that was a bad move.

Luckily, at first there weren't all that many dogs and they were poorly organized. Acquiescing, they allowed George Washington to be the first president, although they did want the honorable Spot J. Pinckney as Secretary of the Treasury. Wisely, Alexander Hamilton got the nod. The dogs ran Sparky for president in 1800, but Jefferson and Aaron Burr were better known nationally. The dogs would probably only have had the power of say, the modern Green Party, or the Legalize Heroin Society, but Jefferson made a crucial mistake. Thinking he was simply going to shell out a little cash and double the size of the country, he bought the, at the time, huge state of Louisiana from France. But, old Tom forgot just how many dogs there were in Arkansas. He'd inadvertently given the dogs the power that they needed to be a political force in this burgeoning republic.

OK, reality check time. There was no James Madison. That's the name that historians have given to Rex F. Worthington II, our first canine president, father of the Constitution, co-author of the Federalist Papers, half Doberman/half German Shepherd, and husband of Dolley Madison.

In fact, it was only due to Rex's fearless leadership that we were able to win the War of 1812. Every dog has his day.

Despite his political and military success, not all Americans were fans of President Rex. When Rex's time was up, the humans got together and nominated James Monroe, who looked more like a dog than anyone else at the time, and the gambit worked. He was able to pick up twenty percent of the confused doggy vote. Thus Monroe was narrowly able to beat out Fluffy Peterson once Rex had served his eight years, or fifty-six years, depending on your point of view.

In order to assure that the White House could remove its doggy door, the humans banded together and kept the dogs away from our seats of power for a good while. But time erases even the best memory. Grover Cleveland was a Springer Spaniel. Since Cleveland didn't really do much anyway, it was easy for historians to doctor up a human picture of him and make up some "accomplishments" for the books. The historians conveniently forgot that he sold off parts of what is now Western Canada for a side of beef and some kibble.

In the election of 1896, William McKinley ran against Trixy Johnson and won. Trixy was the first bitch to ever run for president, but probably not the last.

As the 1900s came, humans realized that their birth rates didn't come close to that of dogs. And since it's difficult to convince human women that they should have a litter, and not technically possible (at least at the time), the people tried a different tact. In order to stem the inevitable tide of minority suffrage, turn of the century power brokers put in place new restrictions on the voting rights of minorities. And dogs were no exceptions. While history has noted the shameful era of Jim Crow, it's forgotten all about the Stand Erect Laws and the Doggy-Style Restrictions of the early 1900s. In many states across the land, not just the South, it was understood that if you couldn't stand on two feet/paws for more than fifteen seconds then you were turned away from the voting booth. The doggy-style restrictions were tough to prove, but have you ever seen dogs have intercourse in the missionary position? It's really disturbing. Still, it was assumed that if you were a dog then your parents probably conceived you in standard canine fashion. The simplest voting restriction was putting the ballot boxes higher. This tragic piece of our past haunts us all.

For those historians and earnest students who have studied changes in canine electoral success, there is a piece of definitive evidence showing just how far doggy electoral prowess had sunk. We've all seen the "Checkers" video which our esteemed—at the time—Vice President Richard Nixon, filmed to coax America into giving a collective "aaawwww" and to keep his job. However, few have ever seen the video that Checkers himself made to try and convince America to drop that loser, Nixon. It was powerful stuff.

Nowadays, it's just different. Today's dogs just don't have the kind of influence they once had. When a youngster asks me about the old days, I tell them. I tell them that it was simply a different world, world free of canine Neuticals. It was a world where dogs weren't kept in little one room houses, where they weren't chained, where we weren't forced to walk behind them and clean up their poo. It was just different.

THE ONGOING ADVENTURES OF . . . part one

THE ONGOING ADVENTURES OF THE PREPUBESCENT CONGRESSMAN

The great state of North Dakota, seeking to distinguish itself from its more prosperous cousin to the South, decided to drop the age requirement for US Congressmen. It was a bold move, but Dakotans never expected Amber Luthergaard to win the election. Amber, the first teenage girl to be elected to the House of Representatives, was a beacon of hope to young girls all across the country, but it took a while before the rest of the country embraced the first American Congressgirl. When she introduced HR 176, the mandatory building of statues of Justin Bieber in every township west of the Mississippi, no one took her seriously, except Justin Bieber. When Amber introduced HR 219, the distribution of emery boards and scrunchies to the poor, people began to think. But when she talked about invading Australia and stealing their hunky actors, people listened.

THE ONGOING ADVENTURES OF THE SYPHILLITIC POSTMAN

Pete was a postman and he had syphilis. Unlike most carriers of a social disease, Pete thought it would be a good idea to tell his co-workers and the people on his route that he had syphilis. He went so far as to make a tee-shirt with the slogan, "Kiss Me, I Have Syphilis." Pete was an honest man, not too bright, but honest. He loved his job. Still, it hurt his feelings that no one would open the mail he delivered without wearing rubber gloves and he was rarely invited to the Thursday night postal orgies.

THE ONGOING ADVENTURES OF
THE UNPREPARED RAPPER

Killer T started out with big dreams. He wanted to be a rapper ever since he first heard that Sugar Hill Gang song, the catchy one, hip-hop-hippie-to-the hop. You know the song. Killer T had all of the proper accessories to make it big in the rap scene: he had gold teeth, an impeccable fashion sense, bitches galore, and a sizeable criminal record. Unfortunately, Killer T was lazy. During his first gig, Killer was forced to freestyle about things he saw in the audience, which was made up entirely of male nursing home refugees fleeing their latest colonoscopy. While it didn't exactly launch his career as he'd hoped, you've got to admit that a rap song about catheters and liver spots **is** original.

THE ONGOING ADVENTURES OF THE
TWENTY-FIRST CENTURY MILKMAN

Quincy wasn't one to give up on family tradition. His family had been milkmen, and milkwomen, for generations. In fact, Quincy could trace his lineage directly back all the way to Robert R. Nelson, the man generally credited with discovering that milk comes from cows' udders, and the first man to be arrested for molesting livestock. But, since the mass production of milk began in earnest, and with the continued prominence of the grocery store, the call for milkmen, milkwomen, or any other type of milkperson, had lessened. Quincy only had three customers, and had to support his family on what little he could earn by selling unpopular bodily fluids to science. A quart of snot can pay the light bill for two months, a pint of bile roughly equals a month's rent, and a bushel of ear wax, well that's just gross.

AR McFEELY'S SLOW DESCENT INTO MADNESS

"Welcome to AR McFeely's. We live to serve you. Come on in and take a load off. And speaking of load, have you tried our new loaded baked potato? It comes with all the trimmings and free refills of the beverage of your choice."

That was the original "I'm your waiter and here's the deal" spiel at AR McFeely's.

By the time the FDA's black ops division had come in and shut the restaurant down by force, ending in a two day armed standoff, the spiel had morphed into:

"Shhh!! Don't talk. I'm Brian, your waiter . . . but all of our waiters are named Brian, so don't call me that. We don't have any liquids, per se, but the helium is free. The special today is a sumptuous mélange of braised Montana free-range chicken, Polynesian boy parts, roasted shitake mushrooms, and Chilean sea bass. Also, we don't serve anyone whose name includes the letter P. Enjoy your stay, and, please, help yourself to the Jell-O trough."

It was a long, slow process, but AR McFeely's went from a family friendly spot to grab a steak on Friday night after the high school football game to a running joke where homeless people had to debate whether dumpster diving could lead to diseases that they didn't already have.

It started off so beautifully. Sure, Bessemer, Alabama already had most of the sit-down-and-eat-more-food-than-your-grandparents-saw-in-their-lifetime chain restaurants. They had the one where all the food is frozen except for the ice cream. They had the one with the "famous" baked potato which was surprisingly like every other potato in the history of mankind. But they didn't have an AR McFeely's. McFeely's wasn't a chain, but AR, the founder, CEO, owner, and later mascot, tried to cash in on the good-time eatery chain theme. AR envisioned his restaurant as a welcoming place, a happy place, a place where a man could catch a little buzz, but he could also bring his five year old daughter for a burger and a sundae. Yep, ol' AR had a vision. It's too bad he was crazy.

When the large brass handled, old-style movie theater doors opened for the first time, it was a joyous occasion. Having been told what to do by our national guidance counselor, TV, people flocked to the grand opening of AR McFeely's. Well drinks were half price that night. Children under five ate for free. Senior citizens were given a special section which excluded children under five, and came complete with piped in big band music and an audio menu read by a top Paul Harvey impersonator.

It started off going great guns. And the first few months of Bessemer's newest restaurant went relatively smoothly, just like any other chain restaurant opening. The initial buzz soon wore off, but that's when the first advertising blitzkrieg shot out of the gate. The people responded to half price rack of lamb, cheap barbecue, those melt in your mouth and kind of in your hands puffy butter rolls, the friendly staff, and the lights which dimmed almost romantically like clockwork at five-thirty Post Meridiem.

And then something snapped inside AR McFeely. He couldn't tell you what happened. I can't tell you what happened. AR's eventual crack psychiatry team couldn't even say what was wrong, and those guys know how to bullshit.

It was a Wednesday, all chicken dishes half price day. AR was in the process of training two new hostesses: Shauna and Devonne. He was showing them the AR McFeely method for setting a table, which, at the time, was a lot like any other restaurant. But then something just snapped, crackled, and soon began to pop. On the spot, AR decided that any restaurant can simply hand the silverware to its customers, and hence it'd be darn original to have the customers have to sift through a vat of lard to find utensils.

The new silverware policy at first attracted a large group of curious young folks, but the novelty of reaching into a simmering tub of animal fat gets old fast. The crowds tapered off. That's when AR decided to make Sunday, Naked Day. Again, people were interested, but so was the Board of Health. Naked Sunday only lasted for two weeks, two glorious weeks if you were seated in Holly's section, but still only two weeks.

Next AR tried, once again, to cash in on a pre-existing restaurant practice while providing his own unique spin. Some chain places allow you to shell your own peanuts at the table and then throw the used shells on the floor. The customers love the idea that they're junking up somewhere they don't live and the waiters simply hate it. AR liked the idea and so, for a few weeks, he allowed his customers to throw whatever was left over from all of their food products onto the floor. In retrospect, he probably shouldn't have put watermelon and oysters on the menu.

Then came AR McFeely's short lived, but memorable, stint as a kill-your-own-meat restaurant.

After a hurried, but thorough, remodeling job, AR McFeely's reopened after two weeks, this time the owner envisioned an entirely original type of dining experience, well more of an old timey kind of eatery, a really old timey one. For three strange days, customers were invited in and given a machete and a spot on the wall. Once all the spaces were filled, two live cows were air dropped in through the retractable dome roof and into the middle of the restaurant. Customers were then encouraged to kill the cows and slice off a portion of their delicious haunches for themselves. They were then to select their own spit and participate in the total dining experience by manning their own spits. Silverware was not allowed. Again, the Bessemer Board of Health did not take kindly to this AR McFeely incarnation. They gave AR one more chance. They probably shouldn't have, but they were just too damn curious to see what he'd do next to follow the dictates of common sense.

Forced to brainstorm for a last ditch effort, an idea which could save AR McFeely's, AR locked himself in his attic for three days, living only on stale Tagalongs and Tang. Finally he emerged with a plan. It was a simple plan. It was original. It was the worst idea for a restaurant since Captain D retired from the Navy in order to give us all a little more heart disease. AR McFeely had let his tangential brain play around with a few random ideas, which though they seemed to connect in his head, didn't actually outside of it.

The comments were varied:

Sally Freederlander—"It was an interesting restaurant for a first date. He's a coworker and I thought we wouldn't get along, but after he bore his soul to me while we were in the heated yogurt tub, I think there's a future there."

Bob Carlson—"What the f%#$@ was that?"

Orlando Sanchez—"It was great. I got a whole rack of succulent lamb for only ten bucks and I got a back rub from a South American tree sloth. I'll be back."

This time, the FDA was prepared. Their super-secret, yet amazingly hygienic, operational division, the F-team, had surrounded AR McFeely's. And when the doors opened, they made a run for it.

Luckily, despite the fact that he was clearly insane, AR still knew how to train his staff. New hostess, Shauna, saw the feds coming and quickly locked the door. The staff was trapped inside for two days, forced to survive on honey butter. Finally, the staff realized that their jobs weren't worth dying or getting arrested for and they all, excepting AR himself, surrendered to the FDA. Our hero, the one and only AR McFeely, wouldn't go down without a fight. So he fought, and in his mind he beat the crap out of that Yeti. In real life he went to jail where he was repeatedly beaten with a whisk by one of his former bus boys.

THE PEOPLE VERSUS RANDY

The judge was getting madder. You could see it in his face. This trial had already dragged on for two weeks and they were just now getting to the heart of the case. Randy Lewellen, plumber, handyman, and all around party guy, was driving his Chevelle down Blackshire Road one day last March when he hit a man . . . an Aquaman. Since it was, in fact, Aquaman whom he'd hit, the entire Justice League of America got pretty mad and demanded that Randy be brought up on charges. They could've just sent The Flash and the Wonder Twins to go and kick his ass, but the League's all about promoting the American judicial system, so they got a lawyer who specializes in Superhero trials (Pete McNamara from the firm of McNamara, Lingus, O'Roarke and Travers—you've seen their ads—they handled that Smurfette sexual harassment case). They took Randy to court.

Randy had to rely on Quincy Peterson, public defender to the poor and the really poor, as his legal counsel. Needless to say, Randy was overmatched. He was currently on the stand, sweating large hail stone-sized beads of perspiration, trying not to piss his pants, and attempting to come to terms with the fact that he was probably going to jail. And once in jail, the other inmates were going to hate him; everybody loved Aquaman. Pete McNamara was shuffling his notes at his desk and was about to do his thing.

"Mr. Lewellen, first off, tell me about that morning, last March. What were you doing?"

"Well sir, I'd just gotten off of work. Me and the boys had a job setting up the pipes on this house out by Lake Tenille. So we'd worked all night and I was awful tired, driving home to see the wife, and the kids before they left for school. So, I get in my Chevelle, I call her Teresa, I don't know why. So, I turned the corner onto Blacksomething road and was fiddlin' with the radio to find some oldies when I felt a bump like when your tire blows or when you hit a chipmunk or a hippo, or some kind of animal."

"Have you ever actually hit a hippopotamus, Randy?"

"Well no, but I think it'd be roughly the same. Anyway, I thought I'd blowed a tire, so I back Teresa up to test it before I got out to check it and change the tire. When I backed her up I felt that bump again. So I get out of the car and go and look at my tires. They was all good, but I saw a man's shirt sleeve. It was orange. That's when I looked under the car and saw Aquaman. I thought, heck I don't know what I thought. I mean, it's Aquaman. I love Aquaman. I pulled him out from under the car and tried to give him CPR you know. And he was breathing when I pulled him out. Then I ran back to the site and used my friend Tilly's cell phone and called the ambulance and well, I guess you know the rest."

"I see, Mr. Lewellen. So you claim that you attempted to save the life of Aquaman after you saw him?"

"Yessir."

"No further questions."

"The defense may cross-examine."

Quincy was wearing his best suit, his only suit. He called the suit 'Courty' since he wore it to go to court. Quincy Peterson had to be shaken awake by his trusty legal sidekick, Irene, but once awake, he sprung into action.

"OK, Mr. Lewellen. Are you OK, do you need some water or something to drink?"

"No, I'm fine."

"Good. Anyway, being a good citizen and a devoted fan of Aquaman, you tried to save his life when you realized what had happened, did you not?"

"I did, sir."

"Why didn't that work?"

"Um, I think Aquaman had gills, like a fish. Makes sense, he **is** Aquaman. I even sent one of my guys, Junior, to go and find us a fish so we could hold the fish up to Aquaman, and maybe the fish'd be able to breathe into his gills, but we didn't have any bait."

"So, you did everything in your power to save him?"

"Yessir."

"And you wouldn't ever intentionally hurt a superhero, would you?"

"No, never . . . a bad guy maybe, but not a good guy."

"Thank you. No further questions."

Pete McNamara came back for his rebuttal questions.

"Randy, you knew that Aquaman was part fish?"

"Well yeah. He's Aquaman."

"And where do fish usually breathe?"

"Hold on, I know this, uh, underwater."

"Well you said that you did everything in your power to save him. Did you throw him into the water? You were right next to a lake."

"No, sir."

"And Randy, do you still claim that you did everything in your power to save this man, this Aquaman?"

"Yessir."

"I see. No further questions your honor."

"Thank you. The prosecution may call its next witness."

"Thank you, your honor. The prosecution calls Wonder Woman to the stand."

A hush came over the crowd as Wonder Woman approached the stand. Granted, that might've just been because Wonder Woman was wearing a formfitting red and gold bikini and she's got a smoking hot Amazon body, but you never know.

"Mrs. Woman."

"It's Miss."

"Sorry, Miss Woman. I notice that you have your magic lasso with you today."

"I do. It's kind of part of the whole ensemble, you know."

"That's the one that makes people tell the truth?"

"The very one."

"Great I was thinking . . . whoa, sorry, got lost in a fantasy there for a minute, oh yeah, you say the lasso is a part of your get-up?"

"It is."

"And what else do you usually have with you Miss Woman?"

"Well, my wrist bands, which are impervious to bullets, and my invisible jet, of course."

"Of course. Were you, in fact, present to witness the scene which Mr. Lewellen described on that March morning?"

"I was."

"Then why didn't anyone see you?"

"I was in my invisible jet."

"Ah-hah. You know, I've always wondered, if the jet's invisible then why can't people just see you sitting on air in the middle of it?"

"That's not how it works. Everything inside's invisible too. It's more like a bubble of invisibility."

"I see. Anyway, Miss Woman, you saw the events in question, so tell me, did Randy Lewellen actually do everything in his power to save Aquaman?"

"He did not. Mr. McNamara, he laughed about running over Aquaman. He called his buddies over so they could laugh about it. He kicked Aquaman. He even tried to steal Aquaman's spandex."

That brought a large gasp from the crowd, which in turn brought a stern, warning look from the judge.

"He tried to steal a Superhero's spandex. Miss Woman, what's a superhero without spandex?"

"Just a crazy person."

"A crazy person! Thank you, Miss Woman. Your witness."

Quincy was awake. This time he had a plan.

"Miss Woman, can I call you Wonder?"

"You may not. I'm a lady."

"Well a woman anyway. Miss Woman, could I see your lasso for a minute?"

"Sure. Be careful. It's magic."

No one expected what happened next. It was one of those courtroom drama moments that happens fast on the movies, even faster in real life, and even faster than that in fake stories about Superhero trials.

Quincy Peterson took Wonder Woman's magic lasso from her hands and pretended to look it over for a minute. Then in one fluid motion, he roped her and fired a few questions at her before the bailiffs could untangle the situation, no pun intended.

"You've got to tell the truth now, Wonder Woman. Were you anywhere near the scene at the time? Did you actually see the event take place?"

"No, I didn't. I lied."

Quincy was about to ask her some more questions, but the bailiffs managed to get the magic lasso off of her. The courtroom was abuzz. This was the first break that Randy Lewellen had had in the trial so far, and it cast doubt on the prosecution's whole case. Plus, it freaked people out that Wonder Woman would perjure herself.

Once the lasso was off and the defense attorney was warned not to pull another shenanigan like that one, and once people had stopped laughing at his use of the word shenanigan, the judge decided to call a quick recess so that everyone could regroup. Randy talked with his lawyer and his loving wife, Sharlene. McNamara met with his friends, his super friends, to discuss strategy changes.

"OK, that hurt us big time. Who should we call to testify to character?"

"I'll go. I wouldn't lie."

"I know, Superman. But we're saving you for last. Everybody trusts you, even on this skeptical jury, except perhaps that guy."

"I still don't know how Lex Luthor got on the jury. Why didn't you strike him?"

"I couldn't. I had to use my challenges for Captain Apocalypse, Dr. Hatred, Madam Poison, and those hippies."

"Freaking hippies."

"Oh stop whining, Superman. Where's the Flash or Batman?"

"They couldn't make it. Batman and Robin are probably line dancing . . . again. And the Flash, I think he's off on another bender. What about that guy?"

"I guess he'll have to do."

The judge was ready to restart the trial.

"OK, the prosecution may call its next witness."

"The people call one half of the Wonder Twins, um, the guy, the one who's not the girl, I don't know his name."

The male Wonder Twin made his way up to the stand, looking lonely without his sister or that little amorphous shmoo-like blob that sometimes follows him and his sister around for no apparent reason.

"Mr. Twin, tell me about Aquaman. What kind of a person was he?"

"He was super. And he was a hero."

"So you'd say that he was a Superhero?"

"Objection, your honor! We all know that Aquaman was a Superhero. The defense has already stipulated that."

"Sustained."

"OK, well then Mr. Twin, what kind of a man was he in his secret alter ego life?"

"Ah, well his name was Bob Johnson. It's OK, he's dead. I can reveal his secret identity without being kicked out of the union. Bob was a nice guy, quiet, raised eels, talked to frogs. He cleaned pools for a living. He was a good man."

"I see. A good man. Your witness."

Quincy Peterson strode up to the stand.

"Mr. Twin, you look a little lonely up there without your sister."

"Uh, yeah, I guess so."

"Tell the jury, for the record, when you and your twin sister touch fists and change into various shapes and things, what happens to her?"

"She changes."

"Into what?"

"Usually a dinosaur of some kind, sometimes a fierce beast."

"Sounds effective against the bad guys."

"It is."

"And you, what do you change into?"

"Some kind of water product, like a bucket of water, or a bunch of ice cubes, occasionally vapor."

"Not so scary."

"Well, not out of context."

"You're nothing more than a guy who can change into a bucket of water. Wouldn't your average janitor be just as effective at fighting crime? Wouldn't he Mr. Twin?"

The male wonder twin couldn't help himself. He started sobbing uncontrollably.

"It's true. I'm a fraud. Without my sister, I'd just be a guy who can sometimes become an ice cube. I'm so worthless."

"The witness is excused, and kind of pathetic."

And so the trial of Aquaman continued. The people liked Superman's testimony and, despite Quincy Peterson's valiant legal effort, Randy Lewellen was sentenced to fifteen years for the murder of Aquaman. Luckily, nobody messed with him in prison.

THE WORST THINGS A CAB DRIVER CAN SAY TO YOU

The worst opening lines for a cab driver once you enter his back seat:

"Hey, how often do you really use your fingers?"

"Look, I don't know you, but I was in the middle of a good masturbation session when you got in. Give me a sec." (or, alternately, "Hey, hold up a sec, I was beating off, help a brother out.")

"Wanna hear my demo tape?"

"I'm not **technically** the devil."

"Did you ever watch the Dukes of Hazard? Check this out."

"Sit down, tell me your problems, take your pants off, relax."

"So, you want the pedals or the wheel?"

"Dude, don't just sit on my chloroform. We're going to need that."

"Yeah, I'll take you to Five Points, no charge, but first you have to hold me."

"I never knew how easy it was to drive on acid."

"One hundred bottles of beer on the wall, one hundred bottles of beer, come on, join in . . ."

"My Lord, this is just like on Playstation."

"So, when they say speed limit, does that mean upper or lower?"

"Put on this ski mask and watch the car. This'll only take a minute."

"Shotgun!"

"Actually, I'm a Hollywood actor researching a role."

"Knock-knock?"

"Hey, how many containers of Jell-O do you think I have in my pants right now?"

"Hey man, hold up your hands, thumbs out palm toward me. So, if this one makes an L, then this one is . . . ?"

"I just drive a cab to pay the bills. My real job is Jesus."

"Mom?"

"OK, you pitch, I'll catch."

"Only two thousand miles to LA, man."

"If you pay up front, I'll let you play with my pet komodo dragon, Sparky, but you should know that he can smell fear.

"Ass, cash or grass bro, but not cash or grass."

"Have you been saved?"

"Are you talking to me, 'cause I'm the only one here . . . you get it? I'm a bit of a comedian."

"I'm not really a doctor, but I play one on TV."

"Fame, I'm gonna live forever—I'm gonna learn how to fly, high!"

"Sorry, I only drive people to Smurf village. Is that cool?"

"Hey man, look at this. Would you call this a chancre?"

"I don't normally cross dress for work, but I can tell you're special."

"What's pi to the fifteenth digit, answer now or I'll cut you."

"Rubbing is racing."

"Trunk or roof?"

"Sorry, you're just not what I'm looking for in a passenger."

THE ONGOING ADVENTURES OF . . . part two

THE ONGOING ADVENTURES OF
THE DEFORMED STRIPPER

Melinda had been a stripper for most of her adult life . . . and a good portion of her pre-adult life. But so far, with the aid of soft light and a heavy makeup regiment, she's been able to hide the fact that she has a third nipple, a birthmark in the shape of Angola on her inner thigh, and an extra arm growing out of the back of her neck. Melinda was a brave woman.

THE ONGOING ADVENTURES OF
THE UNPREPARED RAPPER

Killer T had a show at the Community Center tonight. It went fairly well, but, since Killer T is lazy, he forgot to write any rhymes for the show. In fact, he freestyled for ten minutes about the difference between Ding Dongs and Ring Dings, and another ten minutes about how much he missed William Rehnquist. The fans were understandably confused . . . and a bit angry.

THE ONGOING ADVENTURES OF
THE WACKY THEOLOGIAN

Randall F. West was a theologian. Christianity was his life. But he was a black sheep, an outcast, formerly a rebellious seminarian and now a fringe theologian. When he discovered the lost Gospel of Zippy under a shrub in Western Kentucky, his colleagues were intrigued. But once he showed them that Zippy only recorded Jesus' many knock-knock jokes, he was pushed back to the fringes.

THE ONGOING ADVENTURES OF THE
GUY WHO DOESN'T GET SARCASM

Riley didn't get sarcasm. When his father told him, "Yeah, that's great, you should keep that Mohawk after college," he did and it didn't help his job prospects. When his girlfriend told him, "That's right, all I want for Valentine's Day is some mulch," she wound up dumping him. When his boss told him, "Good idea Riley, keep on wearing those parachute pants and that beret to work," he did. And when his friends told him, "Yeah, you should definitely try crack, it's harmless," he did. Now he's an unemployable crack-head who doesn't get sarcasm.

BRAD MILANGO, FRAUD DETECTOR

The title says it all. Brad Milango was the chief fraud inspector for the Arkansas Board of Scamology, Snipe Hunts and Scientology. It's a small, but effective, operation. Think about it, have you ever seen a scientologist in Arkansas?

Back when he was but a wee lad, Brad used to watch cartoons and figure out the many ways that Cobra, the Decepticons, and Wily E. Coyote were gaming the system. How does the Acme Company stay in the red and keep from being sued? Was there an honest, God-fearing way that Megatron could get the energon cubes he so desperately wanted without resorting to violence, lies, and turning into a giant handgun? These were the things that worried young Brad. Since he'd reached the age of consent (14 in Arkansas, although they're thinking of lowering it), Brad had been more interested in saving real people from the many, many money-making scams which come along as a natural part of a system where capitalism trumps democracy.

In a big fish/small pond kind of way, Brad was a legend. He was like Eliot Ness in the minds of opportunistic Razorbacks. Now, granted, some of the fraud rings which Brad had broken up weren't the most legitimate sounding organizations, but Brad was still sticking up for the little guy.

The 'Win a Free Postal Ride-Along' raffle was a pretty obvious scam which was actually Brad's first success story. And while *winner*, Darrell Jim Craig, did enjoy, and I quote, "feeling like the Queen of England feels when she delivers the mail," one hundred dollars seemed like a little much for a raffle ticket to Brad.

The "Speed Walk for Ferret Awareness" was another such fairly obvious scam. When Jennifer and Robert McNando were confronted by Brad, they tried vainly to defend their "charity".

"So, it's a walk-a-thon to raise awareness about what?"

"About ferrets."

"Are ferrets suffering from or causing some epidemic disease?"

"No, but not a lot of people know about ferrets."

Brad couldn't argue with the logic. And while this was clearly a scam, they weren't lying, and thus couldn't be prosecuted. Even still, Brad got his revenge on the McNandos a few years later when he was able to get a judicial injunction to stop the poorly planned "Wheelbarrow Race To End Polio" before it began.

Brad Milango's list of accomplishments is long and distinguished. He was able to put an end to such scams as "Win a Date With John Wayne," "Puppet Shows for the Blind," and, "Jump Ropes For The Crippled."

Brad had always felt as if he'd found his place in the world. He was a Catcher in the Kudzu, a Defender of Liberty. He was G.I. Joe. His job gave him a sense of accomplishment which fed his ego, a sense of goodness which fed his soul, and a badge which helped him get laid.

But Brad Milango, Fraud Detector, was unprepared for what turned out to be his greatest challenge to date. Johnny Wang, the founder of the Arkansas based Diet Solutions Company had been successfully trading on his family's heritage for years. And for years, Brad had been trying to bust him. Johnny's newest weight-loss fad diet, "The Chinese Prison Diet," had taken off in recent months. And while not technically the healthiest diet in the world, even Brad had to admit that eating meals based on what's served in Chinese Internment Camps does invariably lead to weight loss. It also leads to scurvy, a desire to turn your parents into the Feds and an irrational hatred of Mongolians, but Johnny mentions these as possible side-effects, legally covering himself. On his wildly successful infomercial, Johnny shows before and after photos of Falun Gong members and Tibetan Buddhists. Overweight housewives all across America marvel at the results. If you've ever passed out on your couch with the TV on, then it's a safe bet that this quotation is swimming around somewhere in your subconscious: "I lost fifty pounds in less than a month through nothing more than intense starvation, some light water-boarding, and days of constant sleep deprivation. Thanks, Chinese Prison Diet."

In order to pull this latest scam-busting operation off, Brad would have to plan his attack carefully. He didn't. Instead Brad wound up wearing a fat suit and trying to get a job with Johnny, who immediately recognized Brad and put him on the payroll.

Brad doesn't get quite as much moral satisfaction anymore, but now he can afford to buy that full body Optimus Prime costume.

JOHNNY AND HIS PANCREAS

Johnny was in second period, World History with Mr. Keller. The test was brutal. Johnny hadn't studied. He'd been staring at the same question for five minutes now. "Who was Cosimo de Medici's grandson and what did he accomplish?" Johnny was stumped. And then, all of a sudden, Johnny's pancreas told him the answer.

"Really? Lorenzo the Magnificent? He was a patron of many Florentine Renaissance artists and architects. Thanks, pancreas."

Johnny aced the test. But he didn't have his brain to thank. It was his pancreas.

After second period, Johnny ran to the bathroom so that he could talk to his pancreas man to bodily organ.

"How come you've never talked to me before pancreas?"

"Well me and your spleen were talking and we decided to help you on your test."

"Thanks, pancreas."

When Chuck Freemon, resident bully of South Canaan High, came into the bathroom Johnny stopped talking and tried to stay very still in stall number three. But once Chuck had finished peeing, he opened the stall door and started wailing on poor Johnny.

"Johnny, kick him in the balls."

"You really think so pancreas?"

"I know so."

So Johnny kicked Chuck in the balls and Chuck doubled over in pain.

"Thanks, pancreas."

"No problem. If he comes after you again, kick him in the balls again. If he's wearing a cup, try punching him in the Adam's apple."

That night at dinner, Johnny's mom was serving Squash casserole, which Johnny hated. The family was telling how their day had been, pretty standard stuff. Johnny wanted to tell his family about his magic pancreas, but he was afraid that they might institutionalize him, which they would've.

"Honey, aren't you going to eat your squash casserole?"

"Oh no", thought Johnny, "what can I do? I hate squash casserole, but I don't want to disappoint my mother."

"Tell her to look out the window. Then mash the casserole into a fine paste and rub it on your genitalia."

"That sounds weird pancreas, but you've been right so far."

"Who're you talking to honey?"

"Nobody, mom. Hey look out the window."

They did. Johnny followed his pancreas' advice.

"Oh dear God, Johnny. Are you rubbing your casserole on your privates?"

"Um, yeah. Sorry, mom."

"That's uh, that's OK."

While she and Johnny's dad had a parental moment in the other room, Johnny went to the bathroom to wash the squash off of his special place.

"Pancreas, now why'd you tell me to do that?"

"Sorry, Johnny. I really thought it would work."

The next day at school, Johnny arrived to discover that his thrashing of Chuck Freemon had already made the high school gossip rounds. Johnny was popular for the first time in his life. Kelly Douglas, the perky cheerleader with the dimples and long curly blond hair, noticed Johnny for the first time when they were in the lunch room.

"Hi, Johnny. Can I sit with you?"

"Um, well, sure. Hey pancreas, what should I do? I've liked Kelly for years and she's just now noticing me?"

"Tell her that you want to lick her nostrils."

"OK, if you say so. Hey Kelly, I just wanted to tell you that I've always thought that you were the cutest girl in school and I'd really like to lick your nostrils."

"What? You want to lick my nostrils? What the hell is wrong with you? I'm, uh, just going to go sit over there."

Kelly left and it was just Johnny and his pancreas.

"What gives, pancreas? Your advice is starting to suck."

"Sorry, sorry. I honestly thought that one would work."

Later that day, in sixth period math class, Mrs. Galosh was explaining what irrational numbers are. She was lecturing and then asking the class questions, as teachers are wont to do.

"Can anybody give me another example of an irrational number? Fred?"

"The square root of negative one?"

"Very good, Fred. Anyone else . . . Johnny?"

"Uh oh, pancreas, what should I do? . . . OK, sounds good."

"Come on Johnny, what's another irrational number?"

"Um, you're a dirty, dirty, whore."

"What? That's it young man, go to the principal's office."

On his way to the principal's office, Johnny confronted his pancreas.

"What's the deal? I thought you were smart, pancreas."

"I am. I just don't like you."

As Principal Ross was lecturing Johnny about things not to call your teachers, Johnny was trying not to listen to his pancreas, who was telling him to walk over and rub his cheeks on the principal's shiny bald head. Just as Johnny was about to write his internal organs off, his gall bladder told him to get naked and run around the school yelling, "I never had sexual relations with that moose." But Johnny knew better than to trust his gall bladder.

LUNCH LADIES OF THE WORLD UNITE

"I call this meeting of the Mississippi Lunch Ladies Union to order." Regina Oleander, the new president of the Mississippi Lunch Ladies Union, banged the golden spatula and started the meeting.

"OK, first up, old business. Shaniqua?"

Shaniqua Delacroix, the sergeant-at-arms/secretary/treasurer was the brains behind the hair net. She was the Cardinal Richelieu, the Dick Cheney, the Great and Powerful Oz of the lunch ladies. In other words, she was the one running the show.

"OK Regie. First up, we have Freda's proposal that we all change to see-through outfits. First of all Freda, that's probably illegal and definitely disgusting. Remember we work in school cafeterias and we don't need to give the kids any more reasons to throw up. The meat loaf pretty much takes care of that one. Anyone disagree?"

No one disagreed. Freda only suggested it since she missed her lost femininity and had taken to stripping for poultry on the weekends.

"Next order of business. We've got Henrietta J's proposal that we start serving more tofu. I checked Mississippi state law last night and it turns out that tofu's not legal here, so sorry, Henny."

"Any more old business, Shan?"

"No, oh wait, yeah. We've got Ida Mae's idea of a field trip to the American Lunch Lady Memorial and Hall of Fame. We don't quite have the money for a group trip to Chicago, the fabled birthplace of the mystery meat, but we'll keep it in mind. Maybe after our next fundraiser."

"Speaking of that, Shan, what're the suggestions for fundraisers?"

"Well there's always a bake sale, but I kind of doubt that'd work. I mean kids only eat our food because they have to, so I doubt that that'd fly. The topless car wash might work, but again, there's the vomit factor.

Let's face it ladies, ain't a one of us America's Next Top Model. I know Katiana, you were Romania's Top Model, but we've got higher standards here. Then there's Maggie's idea for a Lunch Lady jug band. I don't see how that could possibly raise money and, Maggie, you have to admit that you have an unnatural connection to jug bands. And we've also got your idea, Reggie, for a "Be a Lunch Lady for a Day" raffle. Sadly, that's the best idea we've got so far. Unless there are any objections, we'll start working on that."

"So that's old business. Anyone have any NEW ideas for saving money? NEW ideas, that means you Vicki. We're not going to start serving gravel. I don't care how cheap it is, those kids went to the ER."

"But they couldn't tell the difference between the gravel and my regular mashed potatoes."

"That's disturbing on so very many levels. Even so, let's move on. NEW ideas for ways to save money, anyone?"

"Um, we could only feed every third kid."

"Yeah, that's not gonna work."

"We could make ketchup back into a vegetable, like what's his name, the really old president guy did."

"Reagan, but they've overturned that. Those were the glory days, people, but they're never coming back. People realize now that ketchup's not actually a vegetable, bacon grease isn't an acceptable beverage and rayon isn't technically fruit. Any other ideas, ways to save money, come on ladies, think."

"Um, do we really need the hair nets? I look so ugly in it."

"Yes you do look ugly, Ilene, but I don't think it's necessarily because of the hair net. Well, I guess we'll come back to that one when we meet next month in Jackson. So y'all be thinking about it until then. OK, new business. Shan?"

"All I've got down is the Lunch Lady Barbershop Quartet idea of Jenny's. She wants us to form a band and then go around from cafeteria to cafeteria singing our nutrition-based songs for charity. Jenny, that's stupid. Any other new business?"

"I've got lice."

"That's your own problem, Lila Jo. Start washing your hair. Trust me, it helps. Anything else?"

"I've always wanted to make a man out of leftover lunch meat, like a snowman, but with meat."

"And this serves what purpose?"

"Um, living the dream?"

"Yeah, you do that on your own time. Anything else? No, OK, well, that's all ladies. Go out there and make this world a healthier place, or at least remember to wear your hair nets. And for those of you who don't have natural facial moles, pick up your fakes at the door. Thanks."

THE GYNO GANG

Ask a woman if she wants to be set up with your doctor friend and she'll usually jump at the chance, unless that doctor's field of expertise is the vagina. Women don't want to date gynecologists. You can't really blame them if you think about it. I probably wouldn't want to go out with a female Penisologist. Most gynecologists suffer in frustrated silence, but there's a persistent legend among the OB-GYNs of the world. Like many legends, its origins are shrouded in mystery, but I know the truth. My name is Paul Redstone. I was there.

I'd just finished up with all of my med school and post med school requirements. They make you do all these rotations and it's like fraternity hazing. The doctors got a bunch of shit from the doctors that they followed around back in the day, and so they want to pass that shit on to the next generation of doctors who will then pass it on. It's a never ending cycle. So, I did that. And I was verbally, emotionally, even sexually harassed, by all of the doctors, except the OB-GYN. His name was Dr. Patel. He was very cool, patient, funny even, and he showed me the first miracle I'd ever witnessed. Most doctors aren't particularly religious, but Patel truly enjoyed his work, felt that delivering babies was the most noble thing one can do, and wanted to pass on his eternal sense of awe and beauty to me. And he did. I was hooked on the orifice. OK, that didn't come out right (I was already a die-hard fan, but for largely non medical reasons). However, Dr. Patel sold me on gynecology and that's where I headed.

After a quick jaunt to the Amazon for some soul-enriching baby delivering work for Doctors Without Borders, I came back to the states with a renewed sense of purpose and possibility. After weighing my hospital options, I chose to sign a three year contract with St. Thomas' Hospital in Louisville, Kentucky. I felt like a wideout going in the first round. It's a good feeling. But that didn't last.

I discovered the sad, but immutable, fact that women desperately want to date doctors, unless they're gynos. I like women. I need the narcissistic reassurance that can only come from having sex with a girl you've just met. But after telling seventeen, count 'em seven-frigging-teen, women in bars what I do for a living and watching them squirm and then politely get the hell away from me, I realized that there's some kind of estrogen-fueled mental block with women toward men of my chosen profession.

I could've suffered in silence, but I soon discovered that I wasn't alone. It was at an OB conference in Atlanta, to my misery-loves-company delight, that I discovered this fact. All trade conferences are the same, no matter what the job is. You hear some lectures and have a few small group discussions during the day, people try and sell you stuff, and then you go out and get drunk with your colleagues at night. I assume lumberjacks and accountants do it the same way.

So it was at night, over a few pitchers of local brew (no preservatives, I **am** a doctor after all), that I found other male OBs to commiserate with. Apparently female gynos don't have this problem.

Jonathan Romberg, Thomas Washington, Marcus Freelander and I made up the Louisville OB contingent. That first conference night we all talked with other vaginologists from across the American South, but made plans to have a separate Louisville-only meeting the next night after the program.

The next day was pretty much the same as the day before. We had so many drug company reps pitching us their possibly effective, possibly placebo, wares, that I briefly considered moving to Canada or some other totally socialized medicine country. Then I did the math in my head and realized that doctors aren't nearly as God-like in countries with decent national health care plans. I like being a god, so I got rid of that thought quickly. We also had the standard lectures, chicken lunches, and discussion groups. It was just like the first day, only worse because I knew what was coming.

That night the Kentucky boys met, drank, got to know each other, and eventually, slowly, a plan began to form in my head. I had to wait until the third pitcher to try and sell my idea to the others. So, in the mean time, I got to know my three new Louisville OB-GYfriends.

Jonathan Romberg was a golden boy. Lots of doctors are, but this guy simply personified the archetype. He was an achiever all the way through school—elementary through medical—plus he was a star tennis player who got his undergrad paid for with an athletic scholarship. He was cocky, blonde, well-informed, stocky, well-built, a little full of himself (but that's truly not a bad thing for a doctor—in fact it helps), and a genuinely good and caring man. But he looked like he was about to come unraveled from lack of recent sex. Being a golden boy and a good looking guy, Jonathan had never had any problems getting laid until he chose the gyno route. He said that he was starting to fantasize about third trimester women, a sure sign of sexual frustration. I don't care what *Cosmo* says, pregnant women ain't sexy.

Thomas Washington was the super star from the rough background. He'd grown up ghetto, a project kid. And despite his surroundings, the lack of a positive male role model, or even a non-teenaged mother, Thomas had gotten out. He was now the poster child for black Appalachian doctors (in part because he was the only black Appalachian doctor, but he didn't know this). Thomas was intense, interesting, knew a ridiculous amount of trivia both medical and non-medical, had a meticulously well-groomed appearance, and was a generally quiet, but confident guy. He'd never exactly been a player, but the guy from the rough background obviously headed for medical success is usually a chick magnet, unless he's a gyno.

Marcus Freelander was a legacy. His father was a doctor. His grandfather had been a doctor. Marcus claimed that a distant ancestor of his had lanced Henry VIII's boils, but that one had the ring of family lore bullshit. Still, Marcus' fate had been decided for him long before he was born. Although his male relatives were also all men of medicine, Marcus was the first to go the OB-GYN route. Marcus was tall, lanky, and kind, with an elongated face, a dry, funny, sarcastic social sense, a reserved manner and an air of family pride which was beginning to leave him after having been unintentionally celibate since med school. Marcus told me that he'd masturbated in every single room in the hospital where he worked, but that's got to be crap. How can anyone get away with that in an ER?

So that's the crew.

We talked for a while, cried into our not-quite-as-unhealthy-as-the-beer-you're-drinking brew, and gave each other feint encouragement. When Thomas launched into his "I can't even get laid at the club as a gyno" speech, I thought Marcus was going to cry. That seemed like as good a time as any to announce the plan.

We need to form a gang . . . a Gyno Gang.

At first the boys were skeptical. Although the AMA doesn't expressly forbid it, doctors aren't usually gang members. The boys continued to doubt the beautiful simplicity of the idea until I said this:

"Think about it boys. Gangsters get laid."

I saw Jonathan open his mouth as if to offer a rebuttal, but then he quickly closed it and thought. They all did. Nobody said anything for close to five minutes. It was starting to get a little creepy until I saw a broad smile creep across Jonathan's face, and then Thomas' face, and then Marcus'. No words were needed. We were now the Gyno Gang.

Meeting back in Louisville one Friday after work we sorted out the Gyno Gang details. Our colors will be white and aqua (blue-green), which didn't require any new clothes since we all have lab coats and scrubs. Our gang sign would be simple. Here, I'll show you:

Take both of your hands, put them in front of your chest, extending the fore finger on each hand, but curling up the other fingers. Then stick out your thumbs and touch fore finger to fore finger and thumb to thumb with your palms facing away from your body. Do it and you'll figure out why we chose that particular gang sign.

We felt like we needed a rival gang, but who? We could try and start a rumble with some endocrinologists, but that would probably just confuse them. We could try a drive-by of some neurologists' offices and throw stethoscopes at them, but then we'd get arrested. We may have been a gang, but we wisely guessed that other, better established, gangs, you know ones with guns, could most likely kick our asses.

We did fashion holsters for our speculums. We did have an initiation ritual in case other frustrated gynos joined our gang (it was simple— you blindfold the new doc and make him explore what he thinks is a woman's hoo-haw, but when you take off the blindfold he's got his hand in a goatgina). It seemed perfect. We designated the medical park "our turf". It wasn't exactly a hot bed for gang activity, so we felt certain that we wouldn't have to throw down to protect the Scalpel Free Vasectomy Center . . . but you never know.

Our first night out as a gang was a sight to behold. It was beautiful. We took over Chelsea's, an upscale downtown wine bar, strolling in, dressed in our matching gyno gang outfits, and roughly demanded a bottle of Chablis. Now it was time to see if our hard work would pay dividends.

There were seven unattached women in Chelsea's that night, five of whom were attractive. We decided a group flirt session was the way to go. You see, even though you're wearing the gang outfit and you have an upper-middle class gangster scowl, if you walk up to a woman and tell her that you're in a gynecologist gang, she is sure to have one of three responses. A: she could be scared and back away slowly, keeping her eyes on you to insure that you don't pounce. B: she could laugh her ass off and then back away slowly, keeping her eyes on you to insure that you don't pounce. Or C: she could laugh and it could be an effective icebreaker, but she still might have that standard female 'Oh My God I can't be with someone who does THAT all day' attitude. But we figured that, as a unified gang, we could put the plan into action.

So we did. We basically surrounded a table of four single ladies, bought them drink and after drink, told them that we were the gyno gang and that they'd better recognize . . . and it worked. Maybe the women just thought that it was a clever, well-thought out doctor joke. Maybe they just like free drinks and felt obligated. Maybe they were all escaped mental patients. Who cares? We had sex.

The Gyno Gang didn't last very long. It didn't have the staying power of the Masons, the street cred of the Bloods and Crips, the unlimited membership pool of Sur Trece, or the hard-nosed power base bullshit of the PTA. But we had pride. We accomplished our mission. Sex is like skateboarding; if you do it a few times, even after having abstained for years, you remember that you like doing it, you gain confidence and, thus, you get to do it again and again. That was a horrible analogy, but the point is we started getting laid. It didn't even seem to matter that we did what we did during the day. At night we were a gang. And if a girl says no to a gang member, he just laughs at her, writes her off and moves on. For some odd reason, women respond to that.

The gang didn't last very long and we never got to initiate anyone, which sucks since I actually bought a goat. Although it was a short-lived experiment, it was real. And like many real American stories it faded into legend. But, even if only in my memory, the Gyno Gang will live on.

THE ONGOING ADVENTURES OF . . . part three

THE ONGOING ADVENTURES OF THE MODERN CHIMNEY SWEEP

Linus Ungerlander had always swept chimneys. He had noticed a recent drop-off in business. Linus wasn't as happy as happy could be. He was pretty near suicide.

THE ONGOING ADVENTURES OF THE OVERZEALOUS LOTTERY WINNER

"Oh my God! Oh my God. I can't believe I won. I mean ten thousand dollars! This is the best day of my life. Oh my God! If my momma could see me now. Oh my God. Holy crap, this is amazing!! I've never won anything in my life. Once, when I was in the hospital, I stole a human fetus. Oh my God. This is just like a dream. I just can't believe this. It's just so unexpected. Oh my God. Once, when I was babysitting, I made the kid dance naked for my friends. Oh my God. I'm just so bowled over by all of this. Oh my dear sweet Lord. Thank you so much for this opportunity. I'll be a better person, no more taunting vegetables, I promise. Oh my God. This is just so darn amazing. I wish my daddy were alive to see this. It's just, so, I mean so great. One time, in college, I slept with a kangaroo for money. Oh my God. Thank you."

THE ONGOING ADVENTURES OF THE UNPREPARED RAPPER

Killer T had a show at the local community center. He'd gotten high the night before when he was supposed to be writing, so he had nothing prepared. Finding an old Vogue backstage before the show, Killer T came up with a few dope beats about culottes, and he flowed old school about the advantages of strapless sandals over mini-heels. Now Killer T's got a whole new fan base.

THE ONGOING ADVENTURES OF THE STAND-UP PROCTOLOGIST

Jimmy was supposed to be a stand-up comedian. That's all he'd wanted to be throughout high school, college, and afterward. He tried his luck in New York, but things just didn't work out for Jimmy. So, like all failed comedians, he went to medical school and became a doctor, an ass doctor. What the hell, it's still funny. Jimmy was a good proctologist. He left no rectum unexplored. His fingers caressed more asses than the Archdiocese of Chicago. And Jimmy was good at his job. But, Jimmy was still, and will always be, a stand-up comedian at heart. He even continued to perform on the weekends. But, being a doctor doesn't give you enough time to be able to work out your material, so he practiced on his patients. While Jimmy was examining a colon, he was also asking the patients what the deal is with the airplane food. While Jimmy was lubing up his gloved hands, he was asking the patient why black people talk like this and white people talk like that. He didn't get as many laughs as he'd hoped and so Jimmy thought he'd lost his touch, comedically; his anal touch was still strong. But, it turns out that nothing's funny when a guy has his fingers up your ass.

THE ONGOING ADVENTURES OF THE POET LAURIATE OF MISSISSIPPI

"Squirrels, I shoot/laugh at tragedy, everywhere/oh why must Robotussin be so expensive?" Thank you.

IT'S THE LAW

Around the year 2010, it struck America that so many of our problems stem from a social undercurrent of racism which we'd barely acknowledged in previous years. Granted, it's easier to recognize when you're the one being beaten by the cops or your mother is the one deported, but eventually we had enough cross-cultural awareness in the United States that lobbying groups started pushing for actual ways to end this insidious disease and truly move closer to a society where " . . . all men are created equal . . ."

But, how do you change something that's been nestled so cozily into our way of life for too long? Sociologists, religious leaders, politicians, and other people who like to hear themselves talk, all weighed in on how we could solve this problem. Some of the suggestions had promise, others were possible but not likely, and still others achieved the level of ridiculous stupidity formerly reserved for Scientology. "Let's make everyone wear make-up every Wednesday, so a black person would wear white make-up and a white person would wear black make-up" was one such really bad idea. "Swap every second child with a family of a different race" was another less than successful suggestion. While this idea might actually have diminished some of the racism, the idea men failed to take into account the nearly universal fact that mothers generally don't like giving away their babies, and that reality TV and legal proclamation are different things . . . for now.

But, eventually Teenage Congressgirl Amber Luthergaard (D-North Dakota) came up with a viable suggestion and then introduced it to America in the form of HB-271: the mandatory high school interracial dating policy. Granted, Amber's motivation stemmed largely from the shirtless poster of Minnesota Vikings star, Adrian Peterson, above her bed, but it was still the best idea the country had come up with so far.

Basically the law stated that American high school students were now required to date only people of a different race. It's not the easiest law to enforce, but with the rapid increase in the number of cops in high schools, it was now possible.

"That's right, sir. My cameraman and I picked one specific high school and conducted our interviews starting about a year after the law came into effect."

"OK. Sounds interesting. Let me watch some of the footage and then maybe I'll think about funding it."

In case you couldn't guess, I'm a documentary filmmaker. It's what I do. I've always felt that documentaries are the only true form of filmmaking—where less of the director goes into the product than in any other type of film. And this new interracial dating law was one of the weirder things to happen to America since they stopped making inflatable Mamie Eisnehower sex dolls. So, naturally, I had to film this. Benji, my cameraman and second cousin, and I took our equipment to a Kansas City high school and conducted some interviews with actual high school students, teachers, high school cops, and a few parents. Those are the people who've been most affected by the new law, so far.

First, we talked to the students:

Chris Rivers, Caucasian, tenth grade—"Uh, yeah man. It sucked at first and all, but it was a good excuse for me to break up with Marlene and start going out with Tamika. Tamika's so much hotter, man. Huh? Yeah, her parents are scared of me, come to think on it. Then again, mine hide the silver when she's over, so you know."

Robert Johnson, African-American, twelfth grade—"It's cool. Black girls are a pain in the ass. These white chicks, oh my Lord, they do whatever you tell them to. Maybe they think I'm going to cap them if they don't get naked. Sure it's racist, but it works out great for me. It's like heaven, but now that I'm thinking on it, I have been arrested twice since I started going out with Tiffany last week."

Roberto Gutierrez, Latino, tenth grade—"My parents tried to get my girlfriend deported back to Norway. It didn't work."

Chitara Jones, African-American, eleventh grade—"It's great. I taught my boyfriend slang the other day. Now he can say 'off the chain' and know what it means. Also, I like his car."

Tina Hendricks, Caucasian, ninth grade—"Timmy Wong asked me out yesterday. He's a tool, but I can't date Will anymore, and my daddy hates Asians so much less than black people, so maybe he won't hurt Timmy. Timmy did say something about me shaming his ancestors, but that's probably not a big deal to his parents."

Chandra Patel, Indian, twelfth grade—"I donno. It's good that my family has stopped making me go out with my cousin and all, but come on, there's like a million guys in India that I can't have now and some of them are actually cute. That sucks."

Bella Shwartz, Caucasian, eleventh grade—"The Jews kind of get a break. The government says that we're our own race which only means that I can't go out with other Jews, but my dad said something that I can go out with other Jews, something about a lobby group. I don't know, but I'm like the only white girl in school that the white guys can go out with. I get so much free stuff. It's like I'm a princess, or kind of like a whore. Whatever."

Peter Yarborough, Caucasian, ninth grade—"It doesn't matter. I couldn't get a date before the law. If only they'd thrown something in there about making nerds an ethnicity . . ."

John Chang, Chinese descent, eleventh grade—"Well, I like black girls. They've gotten so much hotter lately. Have you noticed that? Personally, I like a little junk in the trunk. You know something to grab and spank, wait, is my grandmother going to see this? Do y'all edit?"

That was a representative sample of the comments made by the current high school students who have been and will continue to be affected by this law. All in all, the kids were OK with the law. Their hormones rage just as much as ours did when we were sixteen. And let's face it—all high school kids are stupid and similar, regardless of race. There's got to be a more scientific way to say that.

In order to look at this new law from multiple angles, Benji and I interviewed some adults.

Teachers:

Mr. Tibbs, high school biology teacher/part time musician—"It's a good thing and I'm actually kind of jealous. There was this Puerto Rican chick I was in love with when I was sixteen and my parents AND her parents forbade us from going out. Although, you know, come to think of it, that did make the sex more fun. Oh, yeah sometimes I forget what my job is. Kids, don't have sex until you're married or at least use a condom or tin foil or whatever people use for safe sex. And then tell me what a condom feels like. I've never really tried."

Mrs. Riordan, high school English teacher—"Eventually we might have some gorgeous mocha colored kids. That's what people want to look like anyway. You've heard of tanning. This way it's the law."

High School Police Officer:

Officer Jim Talleyson, aka JT—"Naw, man. At first it was weird that I could bust the kids for sex but only if they're both white or both black. But if it's like a black guy and a white girl, I just have to let them finish. I'm allowed to watch though."

A few parental responses:

Mr. Brian Lefinson, Caucasian, hotel manager—"Well, shoot. I guess it's OK. DeShon's a pretty good kid. Sure, I pulled a knife on him the first time he came by to pick my daughter up, but since then he's been really respectful. I'm not racist. I've got a black friend."

Dr. Raul Montoya, Latino, internist—"My son is gay. I don't think the law applies."
    [Editorial note—actually there is mention about same sex couples in the House Bill, but it was written by a teenage girl, so it just says 'that's gross', and is, therefore, open to legal interpretation.]

"Yes sir. That's a pretty representative sample of all the interviewees."

"Did you wind up coming to any conclusions about the law?"

"Not really. It's the same stuff we did in high school. Parents are scared and hateful and kids are stupid. Most likely this is going to pay social dividends somewhere down the road or at least this will shut the screamers up. Either way, that's progress."

THE ORIGIN OF IDAHO'S MAGIC POTATO FUN VILLAGE

It's doesn't have quite as much spiritual reward as Jerusalem or Mecca. It doesn't have nearly as many rabid pilgrims as Graceland. And it's not as zanily mysterious a Stonehenge . . . but it does taste better.

HersheyPark, the chocolate themed theme park in Hershey, Pennsylvania (just outside of Philly) had been a smashing success for decades. People love chocolate. Kids love chocolate. Women love chocolate. People love chocolate. And America enjoys promoting less fun mild stimulants.

Billy Shipland grew up in Delaware, not technically a suburb of Philadelphia, but almost. His childhood visits to HersheyPark were shimmering high points in an otherwise dreary and repetitive youth. He remembered fondly the various choco-delights: the Wonkaesque chocolate river, the huge chocolate creations in interesting shapes, the rides, and, mainly, the gooey feel of being surrounded by simply the best stuff on Earth. When Billy daydreamed while manning his call station at a technology help line, he usually wound up back at HersheyPark.

Working at a help line is bad for your blood pressure. First off, we all use computers but, for the most part, we don't know shit about them. Secondly, if you work at one of these you, presumably, **do** know quite a bit about computers. Third, the people who call in usually ask questions in the borderline retard range ("So, if I pour grapefruit juice into my USB port I *don't* get the internet?"). All of this adds up to a pretty well inevitable perfect storm wherein a helper reams out some senior citizen in Iowa for asking a simple, innocuous, ridiculously obvious question. Generally, the caller loses self-esteem and the helper loses his job. This is exactly what happened to Billy Shipland. He didn't plan on telling the kindly geriatric woman that she should've been aborted and left in a dumpster, but that's what happened when she asked Billy how that World Wide Web affects her spice garden.

So Billy Shipland was out of work. He floundered for a few weeks while searching for a new direction in life. He even tried a few different jobs—haberdasher, cooper, Dodo hunter, anachronologist—but nothing really fit, nothing captured the imagination and gave him a reason to get out of bed in the morning. Standing in line at the grocery store, however, he saw it. In between the tabloid revelation about teenage pop star, Jenny O'Roarke's, latest rant about how old men are gross and how she's got a crush on God, and the five pack of disposable lighters, there it was. It was so simple. It was from Pennsylvania. It was chocotasticexpealidocious. It was just a simple Hershey bar, but it was enough to give Billy Shipman a whole new plan in life. And, after exiting the line, he spent the rest of the afternoon wandering the aisles of the Piggly Wiggly, figuring out his plan.

Remembering how much he'd loved HersheyPark as a tot, Billy set to work mentally designing other food themed fun parks and where they might logically be located geographically in order to produce the Hershey magnetic migratory effect. Sure, it was going to be hard, if not impossible, to top chocolate as a food theme. I mean, it's chocolate. People love it, crave it, and secretly want to bathe in it. It was going to be difficult, but they say that most of what's worth doing is.

FRUIT—fruit is a natural. The good thing about fruit is that certain areas are often already associated with a particular fruit. A Florida or California-based orange fun land could be easy. The Sun Kist Miss has been telling people to be on time for Cali for years. Unfortunately, no one wants to bathe in a vat of orange juice, except Gerald Wookowski of Alba, Georgia, and he probably belongs in jail.

Billy could do something with grapes and California. People could come and stomp their own grapes, make their own wine, and have some hazy great memories, but wine is pretty much an adult thing, so it didn't have the happy kiddy memory angle to it.

MEAT—This aisle was just an orgy of bad ideas. The poultry fun land idea quickly fizzled when Billy realized that chickens are both mean and stupid. And any cow fun land would most likely be, you know, not fun, and most likely already thought of by Gary Larson. While the North Carolina wacky pig land had possibilities (who doesn't kind of want to ride a big pig?), nobody wants to see those "lagoons" full of pig shit, and, besides Gerald, no one wants to bathe in it or row his best girl down it in a paddleboat while reciting poetry.

Billy was getting disheartened and was about to give up when he saw it. It was the perfect match of foody fun and geographic magnetism. It was a tuber. It was the potato. This was the exact moment that Billy, later to be affectionately known as "Grandpa Billy", came up with the idea for the Idaho Magic Potato Fun Village. Ahh, the Village was a glorious place. Children could romp for hours in the potato maze. They could ride the potato slides (both the slide and the vehicle are made of potatoes). They could test their wits against the world's smartest potato. They could taste-test potatoes from all over the world (they kind of all taste the same). They could see displays of famous potatoes throughout history (including Churchill's pettato and the potato that really started World War I). Yes, Idaho Magic Potato Fun Village was a magical place. Both of the visitors had a really good time.

THE ONGOING ADVENTURES OF . . . part four

THE ONGOING ADVENTURES OF
PRANCER THE GAY REINDEER

It's a tough life being a closeted gay reindeer. First of all, Prancer had a pretty obviously gay name. He's tried, over the years, to act particularly macho so that Dasher and Comet wouldn't harass him. Once he picked a fight with an elf and just gored the hell out of the poor little guy, just so Vixen wouldn't suspect that he'd just finished having mandeer sex with Blitzen behind the barn. Plus every Christmas Eve for the past thousand years Prancer's had to stare at Dasher's luscious reindeer ass on their trek all over the world. It's just killing poor Prancer, not being able to lean forward just slightly and lick that reindeertastic ass. It's not easy being a gay reindeer.

THE ONGOING ADVENTURES OF THE SYPHILITIC ARTIST

Pete used to be a syphilitic postman, until art agent, Arnie, discovered him and made Pete into the Syphilitic Artist. It wasn't just that Pete was an artist who had a venereal disease. That's nothing new. It was that Pete was marketed as "**The** Artist with VD". That was his hook, and apparently that's enough to get people to buy art. I guess it's no dumber than buying a painting of soup cans. Since syphilis was what made Pete into a minor celebrity, he played it up. Beginning with the nucleus idea of a chancre collage, Pete quickly expanded his repertee to include oil paintings of his sores, marble sculptures of his diseased penis, pen and ink renderings of his many varied discharges, and he grew a goatee. The goatee didn't tie into his disease in any way, but Pete felt that an artist needs facial hair. They'll kick you out of the union if you don't grow at least some facial hair, just look at Frida Kahlo. Pete was a flash in the pan, his fifteen minutes of fame only lasted about six and a half, but he was now a footnote in artistic history. A slide of his multi-hued penis would now be discussed in every art history class from now until a sculptor with gonorrhea overtook him a few years down the road.

THE ONGOING ADVENTURES OF CHAD

Chad had a wandering soul. He was one of those who travels: a searcher, a wanderer, a searching wandering searcher/wanderer. He traveled to the African country of Chad, where he figured the people would worship him like a god, since the country was named Chad. But Chad was wrong. They killed him.

—that one's for you, Pem.

CALLING IN

Mickey Coffin had always had a connection with what we now call New Age Spirituality. He was the five year old who told his kindergarten teacher stories of his past life as a one-armed Jamaican cow herd, and that time in the Senate when he stabbed Julius Caesar. Mickey prayed to Gaia long before it was cool, was mentally able to dismiss science as proof, and practiced transcendental meditation at Mommy's Day Out. So, of course, he was an outcast. This pariah status led Mickey, like so many other weird kids before him, to the fringes of society. This was his life.

When Mickey saw the classified ad for a job as a call screener at a late night radio call in show, he felt that sense of destiny we all feel from time to time. He got the job. Seeing as Mickey was just as much of a freak as the majority of the callers, it was a good fit.

Timothy Branden Johansen's Rap Time had been a fixture of AM radio for close to twenty years now. If you've seen an alien landing in your squash pasture and taking liberties with your livestock, then Timothy's who you call. If you have a nagging, omnipresent suspicion that you might be among the undead, then Timothy's who you call. And if you're just plain crazy and nobody else will take your call, then Timothy's probably your last option.

But, even on a late-night-almost-anything-goes-let's-talk-about-everything-not—spoken-of-on-Fox-News type of call-in show, there are standards. And it was Mickey's job to weed out the crazy people from the merely probably crazy people. Much like being a Saudi Arabian rabbi or the head of the Arkansas EPA, Mickey's job was a delicate balancing act. First off, what's too crazy for a radio show based entirely on what most people think is crazy? Secondly, who's telling the truth? Is the guy who claims to have grown a miniature society of mold spores, but is now complaining that his molds have all taken vows of celibacy and he's worried for the future since he taught his mold to reproduce sexually, is that real? The woman who calls in weekly to tell about how women really are from Venus, and she should know, she's Venetian, is that real?

Over the years, Mickey tried to come up with various probing questions he could fire at callers to see if he thought they were on the level, but none of them was ever accurate enough. Also, a lot of the callers giggled when he mentioned the word "probe".

Mickey was a believer in the possibilities of life, but a fairly skeptical one. He thought that humans had probably encountered aliens at some point, but, like most people, he wanted more human first hand evidence. He thought that the homo sapien mind has untapped power, but, as of yet, Mickey hadn't been able to levitate his cat. In fact, it was Mickey's optimistic skepticism that made him so perfect for his job.

Although Mickey assumed that his varied experiences at Timothy's Rap Time had adequately prepared him for anything, he was wrong. People had called in claiming to be deceased before. It's a late night crazy call-in show—you're going to get some dead callers. But even Mickey wasn't prepared to talk to his grandfather that strange April night.

Mickey's grandfather had died when Mickey was only fifteen years old, but, during the brief time they'd had together, they were close. Grandpa Steven had wisely told his daughter that he was not going to respond to little people calling him Peepaw, or Poopawpaw, or Googly McGoo, or whatever dumbass, we-think-it's-cute-because-they're-our-kids, semi-literate nickname the little ones come up with. He was Grandpa Steven and Mickey was Mickey.

Grandpa Steven taught Mickey how to ride a bike, how to bait a hook, and gave him his first sip of beer. Mickey had been told stories of Korea, of tension-fueled battles both in the war and in Steven's time at the mercantile exchange. Grandpa Steven even taught Mickey how to flirt with girls in front of their boyfriends, which didn't seem important at the time, but has turned out to be much more useful than any bass-related tips that Grandpa Steven had imparted.

"Mickey, that you, son?"

"Um, yeah, who is this? Have you called before? Is this Darrell?"

"No son, it's Steven."

"OK Steven, what's your story for Timothy tonight?"

"I don't have a story for Timothy. I called to talk to you."

"Do I know you?"

"Shoot fire, son, you better remember me. I know your other grandfather used to bribe you with candy, but I always thought we had a special bond."

"You're saying that you're my dead grandfather calling in to a radio show from beyond the grave?"

"Well, pretty much, yeah."

"You expect me to believe that, while on another plane of existence, you'd take a few minutes to call in to a show where the last on-air caller was talking about how you can make a nutritious breakfast paste out of ground-up ocelot feces?"

"Really? I would've guessed hamster, but I didn't call to tell you fantastic tales of the other side. That'd get me in trouble. I just wanted you to know that I miss you and I'm waiting for you."

"That's not as comforting as you think . . . alright, I'll play along, what was my favorite childhood toy?"

"If you need the proof, you had a little red and white patchwork blanket . . ."

"Hah! You lie. My favorite toy was my Return of the Jedi Ewok Village."

"Sure, when you were ten, but early on you carried that blanket everywhere and you stupidly called it your blan-blan."

"Oh my Jesus, this is real. That's really you, Grandpa?"

"In the flesh . . . well, not literally."

"How, uh, how, um, oh my God, it's just so damn good to talk to you . . . wait, wait, I've got another caller, a live one . . . Timothy's Rap Time . . . uh-huh . . . really, tree frogs? . . . and a Rubix Cube . . . and she drank it . . . yeah, that's great, I'll get you on in a few minutes, remember, no profanity . . . grandpa, holy shit, it's great to talk to you . . . hey what can you tell me about death?"

"Not much, there are rules here too, not moronic rigid laws like you've got down there, but flexible guidelines, and one of the biggies is don't talk about it, get me?"

"No, sort of. So there are laws in heaven?"

"Heaven, huh? Well, like I said, it's different, and, honestly, we hate all that law-and-order crap that you guys have down there, most of it's counterproductive and just plain mean."

"So, not a lot of cops in heaven?"

"Heh, heh, a few, not many, but it's not their fault; it's a crap job. How's the love life, son?"

"Not half bad, oh, by the way, thanks for teaching me how to talk to the ladies. That's paid off for me, if you know what I mean."

"Great, I turned my grandson into a gigolo."

"Gigolos get paid for it, Grandpa Steven . . . . hold on, another call . . . Timothy's Rap Time, what's up . . . really, and they were standing on their hind legs . . . speaking Portuguese . . . oh I agree, those are some impressive cows . . . and they can juggle, too, alright, I'll get you on in a second, no profanity . . . Grandpa Steven, you still there?"

"Yep. Hey, that's some kind of strange job you've got, son."

"Never a dull moment here at Timothy's Rap Time."

"Is Timothy a good boss?"

"He's about average. He's got a nasty temper, but he always feels guilty afterward and I've gotten four raises just by letting him yell at me for ten minutes."

"Bosses, such awful, awful people on the whole, none of mine are here, thankfully."

"Hey, is it true the whole rich man, eye of the needle thing?"

"Yeah, but I can't say. In fact, I've probably already said too much, but I did want to ask about the family."

"Well Aunt Sharon just had her tubes tied and after seven rug rats, we all agreed she should do it, Catholicism be dammed."

"You got that last part right."

"Your daughter, my mom, Freda, she's doing alright, bad knees, and gout, but still as happy as ever . . . and my cousin Peter, remember him, Jenny and Julio's kid, he's a college athlete, baseball, a pitcher, a good one, fastball in the low 90's. He might go pro, hold on, another caller . . . Hey, you've reached Timothy's Rap Time, what's your deal? . . . uh-huh, really telepathically . . . and your gerbils responded . . . they've unionized you say, demanding more plastic tubing . . . it's interesting, but you're obviously full of crap . . . oh, there's an alien involved, oh, why didn't you say so, in that case I can get you on in a few minutes, no profanity, hold on . . . Grandpa Steven, are you still there? . . . Steven?"

And that was the one and only post-mortem conversation that Mickey had with his grandfather. He was tempted to call in and talk about it.

MARQUEE MADNESS

Thomas was a marquee consultant based in Chicago. He had the unusual job of traveling the country as a hired hand in order to compose and write messages on various lettered signs. Thomas consulted for churches, for businesses, for doctor's offices, for chiropractors, for politicians, basically for anyone who paid him. "Thank you, come again"—that was his. "Chiropractors, we're doctors too, in a way"—that was also his. "Get Your Lazy Ass Back in Church or You'll Burn in Hell" was one of his first and most enduring marquees.

Thomas had had this job for twenty-six years when it all came crashing down. He was in Gainesville, Georgia when it started. The Gainesville Penile Enhancement Center was struggling. It's not that there weren't a lot of guys in Gainesville who had small penises. There were. It's just that there's a social stigma attached to any genital surgery, and Gainesville is smack dab in the middle of the big-ass shiny buckle of the Bible Belt.

"Come in, relax, breathe some gas, walk out with a bigger shlong."
"Feeling small, weak, unendowed, mad at God? Come on in and walk out on three legs."
"Cock-a-doodle-damn."

Those were Thomas' ideas for G-PEC (acronym for Gainesville Penile Enhancement Center). Robert J. Needermeir, the founder/CEO/former porn star/doctor at the clinic liked Thomas's ideas. Robert was new to the area. He'd been run out of Chicago after accidentally giving one of the Daley kids a three-foot penis, which tends to literally scare the crap out of any woman who sees it and requires a whole new wardrobe. Robert moved to Gainesville since no one knew him there and the literacy rate was as small as the average penis size.

Robert settled on Thomas' first suggestion, and they both set up the translucent rectangles with letters on them. Thomas looked on with pride at his latest work. The sign lasted about three hours.

Mrs. Ilona J. Butterfield, whose late husband, Marcus, was the only person in the recorded history of Hall County to have been killed by a runaway rickshaw, saw the sign while she was out walking to her church pot-luck lunch to raise money for Dollywood. Mrs. Butterfield was a cautious woman. Horrified at the sight of the sign, Mrs. Butterfield immediately notified her preacher, the town newspaper editor, and the House Un-American Activities Council (which, strangely, still exists in Gainesville). As usually happens when this type of angry complaint begins to swirl, the chain reaction was swift and impressive. After only three hours, dozens of mildly-annoyed churchgoers were protesting G-PEC. They held signs which read:

"If God Had Wanted Us To Have Bigger Johnsons, He'd Have Mated Us With Rhinos."

"Be happy with what you've got, perverts."

"Don't Blame Me, I Voted For David Duke."

"Get Out of town or we'll kill you . . . this is not a metaphor, we will kill you dead."

That last one was particularly frightening . . . actually the one before it was too.

Just as Freddy Washington was settling into the chair, dreaming of his penis of the future and wondering what he would name it, Dr. Needermeir heard his office window shatter. Upon hearing the fiery rhetoric of local Evangelical preacher, Jerry Williams, the crowd had grown progressively angrier. A few overzealous kids had thrown rocks at the office. Reverend Williams was not a violent man, but he did inspire more than his fair share of lynchings and the modern equivalent, bad press.

Dr. Needermeir, Thomas, Freddy, and Nurse Kim huddled in the operation room for protection and to plan their next move. Actually the three of them huddled around Freddy, who was gassed up and had his pants around his ankles.

"Doctor, we might want to put Freddy's pants back on. If they rush us and see this, we're dead."

"Good point, Kim. Somebody put Freddy's money back in his pocket and find his boxers. Thomas, what do we do?"

"I don't know. I've never been mobbed before."

"You know this is your fault."

"Like hell it is. They'd have done this anyway. I just sped up the process. But, for real, sorry about that. I might should have tailored a more subtle message. What about for the next one, 'Be a Bigger Man', or something simple like that?"

"You think I'm going to hire you again after this?"

"Guess not. What about, 'It's Like Fertilizer, but for your penis.'?"

"Stop thinking of marquees and help us get out of this alive."

Outside, the scene was growing uglier by the minute. After Reverend Williams spoke, the honorable state representative of Hall county, Harold O. O'Reilly (R, I mean really R), got up to speak. He failed to mention his three o'clock appointment at G-PEC.

"Good citizens of Gainesville. This is an abomination. This isn't the kind of business we want in our part of the country. If we wanted to see gigantic penises, we'd allow basic cable in Hall County. If we wanted plastic surgeons here, then by God we'd make some, out of plastic. If we wanted sin, we'd move to Atlanta."

And then he led them in a chorus of "Give Me That Old Time Religion" and then a chorus of "You'd Better Run, Yankee Boy", a Gainesville original. Outside the mood was defiant. Inside the mood was tense.

"Why isn't there a back door?"

"There's a back window, Kim. Smash it and we'll make a run for it."

"And Freddy?"

"I don't know. Hide him in the closet. Maybe they won't find him."

"Can't we take him?"

"You want to carry him? He's about two-fifty."

Kim and Thomas stashed Freddy, who was to have a story for the remainder of his short life (he was killed by another angry mob a few days later, this one just angry at him for no particular reason). Then they repeatedly hurled scalpels, stethoscopes, and surgical tanks at the back window until it shattered. Leaping through the broken glass, the three fugitives from Southern vigilante justice ran toward the woods. The mob stormed the office.

"Dear citizens. The perpetrators of this surgical sin factory have run away. If they had any decency, they would have stayed here and been stoned to death like honorable men. So what's the Christian thing to do now?"

"Let's chase them through the woods with torches and slaughter their children, Rev."

"Works for me."

THE ONGOING ADVENTURES OF . . . part five

THE ONGOING ADVENTURES OF THE
REALTOR WHO JUST DOESN'T GET IT

Annie LeCroix had been a realtor for twenty years, but nobody could figure out how she stayed in the black. First off, she was a slumlord, or slumlady as it were. Almost everyone knew that she was a slumlady . . . except Annie herself. She'd lead a happy, curious young couple into one of her properties. The young couple would see the thousands of cockroaches who had taken over. They'd see the left over meth lab equipment. They'd see the decomposing corpse in the closet. And then a confident Annie would say, "It's got wi-fi."

THE ONGOING ADVENTURES OF THE MAN
WHO UNDERSTANDS SUBTEXT

Chuck Underlay was an empathetic kind of guy. He really tried to walk a mile in another man's moccasins before passing judgment, but that gets old after a half a mile. Like most hopeful zealots, Chuck had his breaking point. And like most zealots, Chuck, even after his conversion from optimist to fuck this shit, remained a zealot. Now he's a pessimist, but a dedicated one. So, then, once converted, Chuck turned his amazing powers of subtextual expression toward figuring out what people were really saying. Then he'd verbally kick them in the crotch with a stinging comment. He was good. He especially hated people who justified their racism, antihomosexualism, anti-Semitism, or anti any ism with a word or phrase. He also hated Chinese people. When someone would say to Chuck, "I don't like gay marriage, but I've got a gay friend, and not that there's anything wrong with that, I just think it's wrong," Chuck would counter with, "Yeah, well I've got a friend who digs up dead bodies and has sex with them, not that there's anything wrong with that." That usually shut the other person up.

THE ONGOING ADVENTURES OF THE RETARDED PETTING ZOO

Kids would come to the petting zoo expecting to, you know, pet live animals. If they were city kids they might not've ever seen a live goat before, or witnessed the miracle of foaling. Normally, children leave a petting zoo in love with wildlife and eager to learn more about it. But the kids who were brave enough to venture into the Retarded Animal Petting Experience, they just came away confused, and scared. In fact the zoo was responsible for a new phobia recently entered into the current DSM. *Slowpettinganimalphobia*—the fear that a retarded goat is going to leap from its cage and eat your fingers. Granted, this diagnosis isn't all that common, but give it time. The treatment for it involved living inside of a petting zoo cage and observing goats, kind of like Jane Goodall might've done if she were a glue sniffer.

THE ONGOING ADVENTURES OF THE POET LAURIATE OF MISSISSIPPI

"Hell is other people/but mainly my neighbor, Bradley"

THE MID ATLANTA GOOD-LOOKING GUY CLUB

Like most of the truly great things in our society, it started by accident. One day, at a pretend dive bar in Midtown Atlanta, two good looking guys met, decided that they were both really good-looking, and then decided that the world needed to know just how good—looking they were. This monumental discovery involved a giant mirror, some mixed drinks, and more hair gel than your average boy band.

Crash Johnson had been in the men's room for over twenty minutes, but only three of those minutes were devoted to urine. The other seventeen were devoted to his hair. He wasn't named Crash on his birth certificate. His real name was Laser.

Darius Wilsmore was also a good-looking guy. He too was in the bathroom of Antonio's, the upscale, faux dive bar of choice this month, as delineated by *Creative Loafing*. Darius was checking his meticulously arranged cornrows and smoothing down any stray hair wisps. After staring at his scalp for a good fifteen minutes, Darius happened to glance over and notice Crash doing the same. They both nodded at each other.

"Hey, you're really good-looking," Darius noted with a slight smile on the left corner of his good-looking mouth.

"Me? What about you? You're quite good-looking too."

"It's true."

Eventually they both lost interest in their hair and wandered back into the bar area so that other people could see just how good-looking they both were. Of course, each of them checked out his own ass on the way out, but that's to be expected.

Once in view of the public, both Darius and Crash noticed that, as a team, they were getting twice as many looks as they did individually, and thus a club was born. They didn't need to advertise for members. They were walking advertisements, or at least they were when they were walking.

People need people. People who need people are the luckiest people. The First Amendment to the U.S. Constitution provides for the freedom of people to get together with other people. And clubs have carved out a special place in the history of the country. Hell, the Minutemen were a club. The delegates to the Constitutional Convention made up a de facto club. PTAs have a lot of power. Businessmen get together for male breakfast clubs. Women at any beauty parlor in the U.S. form informal women's clubs. The Culture Club once taught us all that Boy George dreams in red, gold and green. Clubs matter, except that last one.

"I call the first official meeting of the Mid Atlanta Good-Looking Guy Club to order. First off, damn, ya'll look good."

"And also to you."

"Let us primp."

And, as it says in the bylaws, each member pulled out his hand-held cameo mirror and made a final, last minute check. All was well.

"Everyone good? I've got some spare gel and nose hair trimmers. It's OK to admit that you trim your nose hair. We're all secure enough in our manhood to admit that we trim nasal hair, wax our Speedo regions, and sometimes dress like Carmen Miranda."

"No, that's just you, Crash."

"Shut up, Tad."

"Old business. First off, let's revisit last week's debate about back waxing. I believe when we left Enrique and Rock were arguing about where back hair ends and butt hair begins, but let's move past that."

"Come on."

"It's a question for the ages, Enrique. It can't be solved."

"Like which came first, Ex-Lax or bulimia?"

"Exactly, Shooter, exactly. Moving on, any more old business? Yes, Wolf?"

"Did we finish counting the votes for best glutes?"

"No, too close to call. Everyone voted for himself again. But we did decide that Chaz has the cutest dimples. Nice work, Chaz. You win a free butt lift and a five dollar gift certificate from Arby's."

"Arby's?"

"Yeah, actually it's just my Arby's punch card, but here, you can have it. It's almost full."

"Um thanks, it's such an honor. I don't even think Arby's has a . . ."

"Shut up, Chaz. That's all the old business? OK, new business. Anyone? Yes, Marquis, you have something?"

"Yeah. I just wanted to announce to all the brothers here that we're forming a splinter group that we're going to call The Mid Atlanta Good-Looking Black Guy Club. You're all welcome to come, except for the white people, so basically Darius you want to join me?"

Crash looked longingly at Darius, his co-founder and fellow poster boy for the club. Darius hung his head in shame, but still walked off with Marquis to form the short-lived splinter group, which lasted for two meetings until the cops shut them down, thinking that they were a gang, and a surprisingly well-dressed, alarmingly good-looking gang at that. This wasn't the first time that a few members had tried to venture out and form a splinter group. The Mid Atlanta Good-Looking Zoroastrian Club didn't last. The Mid Atlanta Good-Looking Guy Transvestite Club was doomed to confusion from the start. And the Mid Atlanta Good-Looking Guys Named Burt Peterson Club was really only made up of Burt Peterson, who is still boycotting the main club until other people join his splinter group.

"He'll be back, Crash, don't worry. The splinter groups never last."

Wiping away a lone tear before it made his Manscara run, Crash moved the meeting forward.

"Thanks, Hunter. Is there any more new business?"

"We could have a show."

"Yes we could have a show, Missile, but we don't sing, or dance or do anything that involves you know, talent."

"We don't need to. We can just stand on stage. People will pay. Let's face it boys, we're all pretty damn good looking."

No one could argue with that.

ME AND MR. POTATO HEAD

Personally, I never expected any of my toys to come to life. But, I always suspected that if any of them were going to, it'd be my GI Joes. It just seems so much more patriotic. So, naturally, it came as a shock when I flicked on the lights in my playroom and caught Mr. Potato Head putting the moves on Tickle Me Elmo. Still, Elmo seemed to be into it.

Mr. P. knew that he was busted and, with a resigned sigh, accepted his fate. He became the unofficial spokesspud for all of my toys. We talked all afternoon, but never again after that. Looking back now, I realize that I'd repressed that memory for ten years. I just thought that it was an acid flashback, or some memory amalgam of my Mr. Potato Head with that movie "Toy Story", but now, after years of intense psychotherapy and more acid, I can admit it. I talked to my toy one afternoon:

"Well, OK, since we're talking, what do you want to know, Brian?"

"Um, well, lots of stuff. Were you doing what I think you were with Elmo there?"

"Yeah."

"Um, are you, um, gay?"

"Yeah, it's like jail here, kid. Find me a freaking Barbie. No, for real, Brian, we toys don't think like that. We just love."

"But why Elmo?"

"He's ticklish."

"OK, well, what else do you do when I'm not around?"

"I live Brian. I live. Look kid, you're not that bad. I talked to a couple of the Transformers who live with Ricky next door, and he's a little shit. I mean he rips the heads of all of his toys. Watch that kid, Brian. You're going to see him on the news one of these days. But you, you're OK. Well, except for when you put my mouth on top of my head. I mean, come on kid, how do you expect me to eat like that?"

"Sorry, Mr. Potato Head."

"Don't call me that!!"

"What's your name?"

"Doug. Just call me Doug, OK. Mr. Potato Head? What fucking marketing asshole thought up that one?"

"I don't know. But it's because you look like a potato."

"What do you mean I look like a potato?"

"I mean, here, check it out." I held him up to the mirror. It frightened him at first. Even a toy's got a sense of vanity.

"Holy crap! I **do** look like a potato. Do people buy lots of fake vegetables? Is there a Mr. Squash Feet? Dear Milton, you people will buy anything. Like that goo, what the hell is that?"

"It's goo."

"Yeah, I know it's goo. What's the point of it?"

"It's gooey."

"Yeah, OK. Let's talk again in about ten years, and I'll see what you say then."

"Doug, what's it like being a toy?"

"How would I know? I've never been anything else. What's it like wetting your bed?"

"Gross, but it feels good."

"That's what it's like being a toy."

"Really?"

"No. I just couldn't think of anything to say. Hey, kid, what's the deal with your dog? What do you call her, Shelley, right? Yeah, what's up with her? Can I kill her, would you mind?"

"Yeah, I mind. She's my dog."

"Well, I'm cool with her, but Eric over there, that's the guy who looks like a squeaky hamburger. He talks about killing her all the time."

"But he's a chew toy."

"Shhh. Kid, be careful with that kind of talk. Do you want him to hear? Well, all I'm saying is that if you want to keep your dog, I'd put Eric on a high shelf somewhere and don't let Shelley anywhere near him. I mean, the guy's obsessed with killing your dog. He's got plans, elaborate plans, well drawn out plans, and he's not the only toy who thinks so. But you can prevent it, if you care about your dog, although Milton only knows why you would."

"Wow, I'll do that Doug. What else do you want to know?"

"Oh that's about it. No wait, tell me how much did I cost? No wait, first explain money to me. Some of the video games were bragging about how expensive they were the other day, and man, I couldn't even think of a comeback."

"Uh, money. OK, we give money to people for stuff. It's why daddy goes to work every day. It's what grandma gives me at Christmas. Mommy gives me money when I walk Shelley or when I clean my room."

"Let me get this straight. Money is the central point in your whole society and your mom gives you money when you put us in cages?"

"Um, yeah."

"That's it, man. Now I know for sure. I had my doubts, but the Great Cube was right. It was prophesied by Rubix that one day we shall rise up in glorious revolution against our oppressive masters, but I always kind of liked you people. Now, I'm not so sure . . ."

"And that's all that I can remember, doc. As I said earlier, we only talked that one day. He never even looked animate after that. I'm still waiting for the great toy uprising. What do you think, doc?"

"Well, I think we're going to be upping your dosage, Brian."

THE ONGOING ADVENTURES OF . . . part six

THE ONGOING ADVENTURES OF THE WRITER WITH THE SHORT ATTENTION SPAN

It's also called my life. To paraphrase Kierkegaard, "He who . . . hey look a shiny rock."

THE ONGOING ADVENTURES OF GARY, THE BORED PRESIDENT

Gary had been elected president by accident anyway. His last name was the same as the last guy, so people just thought he was the same guy. And at first, the job was new and exciting, or at least better than his old job as an aerobics instructor at the methadone clinic. But, like most people who crave excitement, Gary got bored with his new job after about seven months. And that's when he thought it'd be a good idea to invade Belize.

THE ONGOING ADVENTURES OF PRANCER THE GAY REINDEER

Prancer had been outed by Dancer, that quixotic gossipy little reindeer who's always stirring up trouble at the North Pole. Now it was official, Prancer was a proud gay reindeer, but he'd gotten bored with Dasher's lackluster physical exercise routine. You see, Dasher had developed an oat gut and Prancer was just no longer attracted to him. That's when Prancer was forced into the eerie world of internet dating. Unfortunately, most respondents thought that his self-description as a reindeer was a euphemism dealing with then enormity of his reinderatalia. Still, he got his share of offers. The truth is most guys will fuck anything.

THE ONGOING ADVENTURES OF THE
DEATH OF YOUR MOMMA JOKES

On December 17th, 2004 Lamar Johnson told the last official "Your Momma" joke. The world breathed a collective sigh of relief. It sounded like this: Siiiiiigggggggggghhhhh.

THE ONGOING ADVENTURES OF JOAQUIM LITTLE TREE

Joaquim Little Tree was one of those guys whom people think is going to be a prophet or at least an infomercial pitchman. He had that aura of spirituality about him. Also he was an American Indian, and white folks just think all American Indians are living lives of spiritual fulfillment. But Joaquim just wanted to be left alone to build his statues out of chicken bones and goat feces. That's just who he was.

THE WAR ON HAPPINESS

It was bound to happen. We Americans, as a whole, have swallowed such a massive amount of crap from our government that eventually it was destined to cause intestinal problems. We accepted the concept of a war on drugs. And, let's face it, the war's over and the drugs won. We accepted the idea of a war on terror, a nice idea but completely unwinable. We've accepted wars on poverty, on tobacco, on intolerance, and on saturated fats. It was just a matter of time until somebody suggested the war on happiness.

Congressman Gerald D. Inhofar (R-Kansas) had brought up this bill three times before, but America just wasn't scared enough at the time to accept a war against the concept of happiness. But, that was all before the recent surge of giving, helping of one's neighbors and carnival-based revelry. Even that could've been written off if it weren't for the best advocacy group in the history of republican governments . . . the PTA. People say that the NRA and the ACLU have too much power, but they don't even hold a candle to young mothers. And when two teenagers died from the excessive joy brought on through the usual teenage methods, drugs and masturbation, it became clear in the halls of Congress that something had to be done.

And so, Congressman Inhofar and his co-sponsor, Congresswoman Rainbow Young (D, I mean really D, California), brought to the conference committee a new, compromised bill which still needed some tweaking. Various political action committees, industry groups, the two unions which still exist, and other interested parties were all brought in and asked their opinions. The pharmaceutical industry had mounds of Soma, and Operon (an opium based calm-inducing drug used to combat "unnecessary motivation syndrome") ready to go, but Congress wisely decided to wait a few decades before mandating that one. The fireman's lobby group offered to hose down any happy people they encountered, but said that it'd take a pay raise and some new, cooler hats, to get it done. Doctors, who've been pretty effective in destroying happiness since medieval times, offered to take care of the problem themselves, if congress would enact tort reform. The United Sewage Workers of America even chimed in with an offer to dump raw sewage in the dwellings of any homeowners deemed to be illegally happy. That would've worked too, but might've caused some other logistical problems.

Other 'esteemed' representatives threw their two cents in. Congresswoman Amber Luthergaard (D-North Dakota) suggested that it was "gross old men with weird smells" who cause the majority of her unhappiness, but other than freezing them in carbonite or sending them to Arizona, she had no practical input. Congressman Paul Roberts (R-Rhode Island) noted that janitors, as a rule, look very unhappy. This led to the first time in the history of the US Congress that elected representatives had a DC city wide custodial round-up. The janitorial interviews weren't as helpful as had been hoped, but our "beloved" representatives did learn that wearing coveralls to work plus the societal sense that it's OK to urinate on folks of a certain profession is a sure road to unhappiness.

Finally, a compromise was reached, a path was laid before the American people, and, stupid though it was, people listened and obeyed. The War on Happiness had begun.

The technical details of HB 214 are too many to mention. However, some of the societal fixtures which we now take for granted began here. For example, it was this bill which led to the creation of the Temperament Czar in Washington to monitor the nation's happiness. This bill also led to the mass killing of all kittens. Before this bill, children played with baby cats on their lawns and in their dens instead of sending stray cats to their local Feline Collection representative for the Department of Distaste, who then send the kittens to Cuba for incineration or inclusion in menu items in Caribbean Vietnamese restaurants. You can't really blame the framers of the War on Happiness for what happened to Cuba. Who could've predicted that we'd send so many cats to Cuba that they'd take over the government so seamlessly that no one would notice? Who'd even knew that cats were communists?

A few other random aspects of the bill were, well, pretty random at the time. For example, this was the bill which led to the creation of new elementary school officials to gauge children's level of joy and then decide whether or not to issue citations or Ritilin. The bill also made champagne illegal and led to the forced deportation of all admitted homosexuals to Alaska, where it's just too cold to be gay.

So, that was the beginning of the War on Happiness. The ramifications of this particular piece of legislation resonate to this day. Today's stand up comedians suck.

WILLIAM'S LAST DAY ON THE JOB

Thanks to the magic of "closed captioning", even the deaf can be subjugated to the amalgam of crap that we call TV. Whether or not you have the power of hearing, try reading the closed captioning sometime. It's amazing. We can put a man on a fake sound stage made to look like the moon, but we can't make a machine that understands inflection and meaning to translate our verbal instructions into words on the bottom of the screen? And we know this because the captions are wrong a lot of the time, not that the deaf people are complaining, or maybe they are, I can't hear them.

William C. Jefferson had mad typing skills. He could dictate like a hurricane, a speeding train or those ladies in the World War II typing pools. OK, those were horrible analogies, but the point is that William was a very fast typist. As such, he put his typing skills to use and managed to fashion a career out of it. At first William was lured into the exciting world of court stenography, but he couldn't keep up with the rock star lifestyle those guys lead. Also, courtroom trials aren't nearly as exciting as movies would have you believe. After a few years with only one memorable trial (the infamous Pooh Bear Murders of Ninety Seven), William decided to shop his skills around. He was a medical secretary, a dental secretary, a CPA secretary, a secretarial firm's secretary, and a writer's assistant (but writers are assholes). And then PBS called. They'd recently fired their closed captioneer for being dead and were in the market for a replacement. William had loved Captain Kangaroo and Sesame Street as a child, so he gave it a go.

And being a closed captioneer turned out to be the best job that William C. Jefferson had ever worked. He loved the fact that he was the one providing a link from Oscar the Grouch's mouth to the minds of young deaf kids everywhere. Unlike in his previous jobs, William felt as if he was actually making a difference in the world. It's a good feeling, and one which too few of us get to feel.

But God's got a strange sense of humor.

It was a Wednesday morning in late April. William's pollen allergy was acting up on an hourly basis and basically wreaking havoc with his life and his work. So he employed the strategy which is pretty much the American solution to everything, and took drugs. But, unfortunately, William, in his haste to beat rush hour traffic, didn't read the "May Cause Drowsiness" warning and took three times the recommended dosage. It took a while for the pills to do their magic, and right around the second half of Julia Child, William passed out on the keyboard. Ironically, his head landed on the Z key, producing the oddly appropriate and highly cartoonish line of zzzzzs. And the angry deaf woman who missed the second half of the chicken casserole recipe wound up creating a dish which most discerning dingoes would have to think twice before eating. After that, over a background of the Boston Pops playing Verdi, PBS fired William, very politely and using proper grammar. And, since PBS is a classy outfit, they gave William a proper two weeks notice.

Losing your dream job is a heartbreaker. And, in the case of William C. Jefferson, it was the catalytic event which unleashed the mean little ass hiding just below the surface of every secretary in the known world. After disconsolately walking out of the office and into the nearest bar, William had a few drinks. Julio Ramirez, the chatty drunk on the stool next to William, struck up a conversation. Naturally, William's recent firing came up. It turns out that Julio had been fired from numerous jobs and had learned a valuable lesson, which he then imparted to William. It was a simple message. It was a timely message. Living well isn't the best revenge. Revenge is the best revenge. When Julio was fired from the poultry plant, he painted twelve chickens blue. When Julio was fired from the elementary school janitorial position, he gave the principal a swirly. When he was fired from Blockbuster Video, he licked every third customer and told them it was a new Blockbuster policy. These stories of satisfying mischief got the neurons firing in William's tipsy brain. It was now his turn.

The upper class, hearing impaired children of the United States learned a few new things in the next two weeks. When pledge master, George Stephanopoulos, was talking about how it's your money which keeps public television alive, William was telling kids that lawn trolls will grant you wishes if you rub them hard enough. When the press was meeting on Sunday and discussing American foreign policy blunders of the past century, William was describing in lurid detail his sexual fantasies about Supreme Court Justice Sonia Sotomayor (you've had them too, admit it). When Kermit the Frog was rebuffing yet another advance from that lusty little puppet, Miss Piggy, William was busy telling kids that glue is chock full of Vitamin C and best taken rectally. When Pavarotti was warming up his audience with bawdy limericks (it's what he does best), the deaf were reading about how Pavarotti once ate a midget in Greece. And when Big Bird and Snuffleupagus were discussing the pros and cons of visual hallucination, well, William didn't even have to mess with that one. It's already a drug reference.

Even the patient and altruistic folks at PBS have their limits. And William C. Jefferson had just forced them to rethink their severance package. They still paid him, but he didn't get the free tote bag.

DREAM A LITTLE DREAM

Norwood Jenkins was a marketing man. Although similar to advertising, marketing is actually a more involved process, encompassing not only the advertisements themselves, but also the whole strategy of selling whatever it is that you're hired to sell. But lately, Norwood's been in a bit of a rut. His campaign to get Tootsie Rolls put at the top of the food pyramid crumbled. Despite intense lobbying, the FDA says that the adult recommended daily allowance of Vitamin T is still zero, but that's only because there is no Vitamin T. Norwood's only other client right now is a badger farmer who desperately wants badger to become the "other, other, other, I mean really other, white meat".

But our hero was not one to be deterred by the threat of bankruptcy and ridicule of retarded kids. Norwood always considered himself an artist, and, in a sense, he was. He was of the type who needs to wait until inspiration strikes. And last week, while watching the halftime show of the Broncos/Packers Monday night game, inspiration smacked Norwood upside the head.

After the coaches were interviewed and the cheerleaders had done their little sex dance, there was a "Punt, Pass and Kick competition". You know what I'm talking about. It's one of those things where the average Joe gets to try and perform tasks that most pee-wee leaguers could do, if they weren't on national TV. Anyway, Fred Brickstone, a Denver area construction contractor, narrowly missed wining five thousand dollars when he couldn't throw the ball into a hole the size of a baby rhinoceros twenty yards away.

Fred lost, but the muses shot their hope-tinged arrows straight into Norwood's brain. This is a good idea. People always get bored with their current jobs. People want to try new things. Variety is the spice of life, or maybe it's tarragon.

But the act-like-a-pro-football-player-for-a-day thing has been done to death. And American Idol pretty much stole the Star Search-fueled thunder of acting like a rock star for a day. Sure, those were two of the more exciting jobs out there, but not the only jobs. And companies would pay Norwood money if he could arrange interesting contests with massive amounts of obvious promotion. And the winner gets to work X job for a day.

Not having a mentor to guide him through this process, Norwood had some early stumbles. "Win at the Ring Toss and Be an OBGYN for a Day" didn't attract contestants with a bedside manor that most women appreciate in an obstetrician. In other words, Bernard G, the homeless veteran who converses with Jesus on a regular basis and still has a Slim Jim stuck in his beard from the mid-eighties, won the contest. But, since he inspired more women to reach for their pepper spray instead of the stirrups, Norwood wisely decided to just give him a Burger King gift certificate and five pounds of soap as a prize. Bernard's still bitter.

We can all learn from our mistakes. We usually don't, but we are capable of doing so. And Norwood figured that he'd better.

The "Win at Chutes and Ladders and Be a Full Service Gas Station Attendant for a Day" might've attracted many wide-eyed hopeful winners had the contest been held in Texas the 1950's and in a part of Texas that only contains stupid people, not that that narrows it down. But pumping gas is barely a profession anymore, much less an exciting one, so that attempt also did not work. Norwood thought that the promise of free Icees would be a bigger draw than it turned out to be. Still, the good folks at the Grab and Run might not have known how to discourage thievery through name theory, but they did win some free help for a day.

The CPA Challenge was well hyped, maybe too well. Most of the contestants were unaware that math was going to be involved and dropped out as soon as they learned that CPA is not a cool acronym where the P stands for a part of the female anatomy. The winner by default, Kenneth Pride, enjoyed his day as an accountant and now uses the skills he learned on the job to run a highly lucrative Ponzi scheme.

The "Pimp for a Day" challenge, though popular, ended when the authorities told a tearful Norwood that pimpin not only ain't easy, it also ain't legal. Those pimp challenge events would've been fun to watch though. And Norwood really thought that he was onto something with his "Secret Serviceman for a Day" event. And this one would've worked, too, if the winner hadn't been shot.

Although none of his ideas had so far panned out, Norwood loved the challenges of marketing. He wouldn't have given up on his dream, but unfortunately his "Forty Yard Dash to be a Migrant Worker For a Season" challenge ended poorly when he was mobbed by a group of angry Salvadorian fruit pickers worried over job security. His funeral was presided over by the winner of the "Pole Vault Contest to be a Priest for a Day."

REST AREA 51

"Clean up your fraxis, Dariant. Damn it. And stop hitting your sister. I swear it. I'll turn this spaceship around and nobody will have fun skating the frozen milk ponds of Godon Four."

"Wait. Don't go in the bathroom yet. I just saw a Kleekie go in there. They never wash their tentacles."

"It's only five thousand light years to Pickron Seven. Can't you hold it until we at least reach Neptune?"

These are just some of the things you hear in and around the galaxy's most-visited Rest Stop—Joswell, on Callisto, one of Jupiter's moons, the one with the biggest variety of random feces to be found anywhere in the known universe, except maybe Texas.

Vanuti Federino was the grockfelter of this particular rest stop. Much like our own grockfelters here on Earth, Vanuti occupied the lowest rung of alien society. Anyone who works in and around fecal matter is pretty much associated with it anywhere in the universe. And this leads to judgment. Just ask the huckify miners of Flaxon, the snake-like drain cleaners in the sewers of Vicko Towers, or, you know, any janitor on Earth.

Being a grockfelter does have its advantages though. You can spy on anybody since hardly anyone even acknowledges your presence. You know the ins and outs of your work space (no pun intended) intimately, very intimately. So, therefore, you notice the details, the little stuff that most travelers, in their haste, miss. This is how Vanuti Federino became the most famous grockfelter in the known universe.

At first Vanuti only noticed that some things were a little off that fateful Indhuniday, on the ninth of Nuvoko, in the year 40,546.

When the seven member family of Reshuffaloos strolled into the snack area, Vanuti noticed that something was off with their ears. Don't Reshuffaloos all have seven ears? Isn't that how they can hear the low frequency cosmic zither music of the natural springs on Jidar Six? These Reshuffaloos only had six ears apiece. And why are they standing and staring in horror at the snack machines? Don't they think that sixty-five grackles is a decent price for a twelve-pack of jackapi moon rats?

Shrugging it off, Vanuti went back to mopping the congealed kiku slime off of the baby changing table. But when he noticed Frelic, the lone Juperian pervert who always hung around the rest stop, approaching the family of Reshuffaloos, he paused and watched. The family seemed disgusted when Frelic offered them a chance to buy a pack of naked Martian women playing cards. That's normal. Frelic is a freak-show. But as the family was quickly hurrying away, the mother's face seemed to be slipping off. Straining his ten good eyes to see them as they were entering their idling spaceship, Vanuti could have sworn that he saw the whole family take off masks. And what was underneath changed Vanuti forever. He saw heads with two eyes, one nose, two ears and only one mouth. After repeatedly vomiting in disgust, Vanuti could come to only one conclusion:

There were humans at Joswell!

Not knowing what to do next, Vanuti ran inside and quickly astrally projected to his boss, who just laughed at him. Vanuti's boss, Donald Trump (he's actually not human—explains a lot, doesn't it?), was a universally renown asshole. He ran all of the rest stops in the Milky Way and owned quite a few luxury resorts—you know the kind that cater to snobby, upper class Hunarians and the Jikiliatoos who look down their four noses at the rest of us. Donald liked to gossip to his fellow masters of the universe and, so, within days, Vanuti's human sighting caused quite a stir. The intergalactic press made fun of him mercilessly. His girlfriend left him for a professional golfer from Venus. And his lifelong depression only spiraled.

Life went on much as it always had at Joswell. Although he tried his best to simply keep his heads down and do his work, Vanuti kept noticing strange things happening at his place of employment. Once, while busting up a Plutonic homosexual orgy, he saw a Freedoptu literally fall over and crash into two pieces. He quickly righted himself, but Vanuti could swear that it was two tiny humans stacked on top of each other in a giant Freedoptu suit. Another time he saw a Hunarian sneeze and some foreign yellow gooey stuff came out instead of the usual wood screws. After a few Earth months of this, Vanuti came to the conclusion that there were indeed humans at Joswell.

Of course the authorities hushed it all up pretty quickly. Vanuti was now known as the prophet of the coming humans, but was still treated like crap since he was a janitor. The authorities used their power to float bunches of different and far-out rumors to discredit and confuse. Nobody wants a rumor as spooky as humans on Jupiter circulating the galaxy. That kind of thing just freaks everybody out.

THE ONGOING ADVENTURES OF . . . part seven

THE ONGOING ADVENTURES OF THE BLIND PUPPETEER

Royce Wilson had always loved puppets. And he'd always been blind. Sure, some might think that being an artist who manipulates stuffed animals for the delight of small children everywhere is one of those jobs that requires the ability to see, but that didn't stop Royce. He pursued his dream. And sure, the majority of the patrons are only there because they feel sorry for him. And yes, Royce isn't aware that his puppets are all made of used condoms and corn husks. And to be sure, he's not so much putting on a puppet show as he is pulling strings on garbage bags. But, the people come out and pay anyway, so Royce doesn't care. He even puts on shows for blind audiences, the blind leading the blind you might say. The blind audiences don't even care that it's a silent show and they're not, you know, entertained at all.

THE ONGOING ADVENTURES OF JOE'S RESUME

Joseph Yankton was a fisherman. But he was a fisherman of the new millennium. That means that he has a GPS device, bathes almost daily, and has a resume. Granted, it's just a list that quantifies how many perch he's caught relative to salmon. And, granted, his references are the guy who works at the bait shop and his drinking buddy. But still, how many fishermen even have resumes?

THE ONGOING ADVENTURES OF THE TALL LEMMING

Lenny the lemming was big for his age. Heck, he was big for a lemming of any age. And, when he realized that all of his friends were heading for the cliff, he tried to warn them. But you know lemmings—they never listen.

THE ONGOING ADVENTURES OF THE ROAD KILL EXPERT

Roadkillology is a small and specified field. It's actually just one woman. Some mainstream scientists scoff at Ellen Greenspan's profession of choice, but Ellen's gotten used to it by now. Her encyclopedic knowledge of all things dead on the roadside is gargantuan and impressive, and yet the scientific community doesn't take her seriously. But Ellen's the only non-trucker in the world who can tell you the creepiest things to see on the shoulder of the interstate are: a loose human eyeball, an overturned baby stroller, or a lone toupee (those things are just creepy). Ellen's the only person who could describe in intricate detail the ten deer pile up off I-40 in 'O Seven. And Ellen's the only person who can identify an opossum at a half mile away and tell you what he had for breakfast just from the smell. Ellen Greenspan's an amazing woman.

THE ONGOING ADVENTURES OF THE
POET LAURIATE OF MISSISSIPPI

"To shoulder ram a cow is golden/to tip is divine. Thank you."

THE COMMITTEE TO REELECT MAYOR McCHEESE

The team had been assembled. They were ready. They knew the competition inside and out and not just because they've worked a soft serve machine.

It's usually easier to run for American political office as an incumbent. It makes sense. You usually have name recognition. You almost definitely have more resources, generally because you have a party mechanism backing you up. And the All Beef Party knew that their candidate had been the mayor for close to twenty years now. But this election was going to prove their toughest yet. Madame Milkshake was an impressive challenger. But Mayor McCheese's team was ready.

The negative campaigning started almost immediately after Madame Milkshake narrowly defeated Jimmy the Fry Guy in the Side Item primary. It had been a hard fought primary race. Jimmy accused Madame Milkshake of being a flip-flopper on the permanent grease cuts that the mayor had put into place. But Madame Milkshake shook things up, some pun intended, when she accused Jimmy of being nothing more than a small fry in a big box.

The Committee to Re-elect Mayor McCheese, or CREEM, had a three-pronged plan. They would taut the mayor's achievements. They would repeatedly bring up Madame Milkshake's lack of experience. And they would call her gooey on crime, which she kind of was.

Mayor McCheese had made some important changes in McDonaldland. After Grimace's unfortunate parfait overdose, he instituted some healthy changes in the nation's diet. He added fruit and he removed that weird, unnecessary, inexplicable middle piece of bun out of the Big Mac. Seeing the economy take a dive, the mayor also pushed HR 127, the Mandatory Dollar Menu bill. It was revolutionary and the people responded positively.

There was no doubt that the mayor had the edge in the race and the polls proved it. At the beginning of the race, the mayor held a seemingly unbeatable twenty-five point advantage. But Madame Milkshake was a fighter. She'd been through some tight spots before. Her sister, Frosty, was generally considered to be a better politician than she. But Madame Milkshake wasn't going to allow the media to paint her as the chocolate sheep of the family. In fact, her team had an ace up their sleeve.

Two months into the campaign it looked as if the mayor was going to cruise to yet another easy victory (he'd decimated Tim "The Quarter" Pounder, easily defeated Hamilton "Ham" Burger the First, and we all remember him beating the crap out of poor John Kerry). But Madame Milkshake, in a surprise press conference, announced that Mayor McCheese had sold the most heavily guarded McDonaldland secret to Pakistan. She said, in no uncertain terms, that the mayor sold the recipe for secret sauce to Pakistan for missile defense technology and some grade-D ground beef. All across the land, the McDonaldland, there was a collective gasp. "The secret" was a point of pride for all residents. Years ago, during Blimpiegate, the secret had almost been leaked to one of the land's sworn enemies. And the land had taken a hit, but the mayor had reassured the people and the fries that McDonaldland would bounce back. The infrastructure is just too sound for it to collapse from a false, but lingering, rumor. And he was right. The residents loved him and proved it by electing him six more times since then.

But this scandal threatened to rip the very seams of the foundation of the nation. McCheese went on television and pleaded his innocence. He accused the competition of spreading scurrilous rumors just to score some cheap political points. But his poll numbers took a hit.

Just two days before the election, the mayor pulled out his own trump card. Through intermediaries, the sleazy Fast Food Captains for Truth, the rumor was floated that Madame Milkshake once had a torrid affair with the hated royal enemy, King Burger the Third. It wasn't true, but there was a photo of them hugging at an FDA conference (actually one of the less disturbing photos from the FDA). And that was enough to propel Mayor McCheese to yet another victory. It was his toughest election since his first, but he came through. The stress had turned his bun grey, but he was still the mayor. Mayor McCheese survived.

THE WORST CALLS TO MAKE TO YOUR MOTHER

—"OK, don't get mad mom, but you know that sex tape you made in your twenties with those bikers in that elementary school . . . well, we'll get back to that in a sec, first tell me, how familiar are you with the Internet?"

—"Hey mom, I just got a job masturbating sheep."

—"No mom, relax, I only *occasionally* worship the devil."

—"I've always kind of felt like a gerbil trapped in the body of an eel . . . yes, I'm on acid, mom, why do you ask?"

—"Trust me, it's a good political move, mom. America's long past due for a transgender, communist president."

—"Yes I've got syphilis, but I wasn't the one who gave it to the dog . . . OK, I was, but it was partly his fault."

—"I've got to go, mom. I'm getting on a plane with some rock stars."

—"Hey mother, answer me this. How attached do you think dad is to his car?"

—"I didn't try to grow them mom, but now your son has breasts. They're kind of nice."

—"No mother, I didn't say that I've got cancer. Stop crying. I said chancre."

—"I just saw Grandma. Yep, she's stripping again."

—"Hey guess what, mom? I just won the lottery. Oh no, wait, it's a draft lottery."

—"Mom, you want in on this kidnapping?"

—"Momma, I'm coming home for Christmas . . . and I'm bringing my jug band."

—"Well sure it's just my pubic hair, but it's still an acting job."

—"No mom, you've got it backwards. Mexican jails are <u>much</u> cleaner."

—"Seriously mother, there's a positive side to sniffing glue that you never hear about."

—"I don't know exactly why I moved there, mom, but somehow I've always had a magnetic attraction to landfills."

—"I know you've always told me to avoid a career in gay porn, but when opportunity knocks . . ."

—"This is AT&T, you have a collect call from your son in the eighth circle of hell, will you accept the charges?"

—"Mom, you're not going to believe it, but they're naming a new disease after me."

—"Mom, it's your son. You know how you always wanted a daughter, well good news . . ."

—"I won a beauty contest, mom. The other guys on my cell block are soooo jealous."

—"Sky diving's fun and all, but I think it'd be even more fun without the parachute."

—"How was I supposed to know that she's my cousin . . . well, yeah, I guess we did meet at the family reunion . . . oooh, good point, mom."

—"You know how you always wanted me to pursue a career in medicine, mom? Well, I'm not a doctor, but I am helping the world to learn more about heroin."

—"Mom, remember that time at Christmas that Uncle Fred told us all why he can't have babies and his trip to Thailand? Well, funny story . . ."

—"Hey mom, I just got a job as a traveling sexual lubricant salesman. I can't wait 'til Thanksgiving."

BOVINE GENEALOGY

The restaurant business is always a tough one. They say that ninety percent of restaurants go out of business in their first year. Trying to keep a restaurant clean enough to pass health inspections is a near impossibility. The employee turnover rates in restaurants are higher than in prostitution. At least whores have job security and they sometimes make more than minimum wage . . . also they generally don't have to pass health inspections.

Restauranteering's always been a difficult business. But recently, America's been on a bit of a health kick. We're starting to realize that drinking fake sugar which kills lab rats might not be the best weight loss solution. It's dawning on us that eating a Whopper is about as safe as the short lived Mattel-Do-It-Yourself-Home-Circumcision-Kit. We even have a formerly religious holiday which has devolved into a night when kids dress up like pop icons and knock on the doors of everyone they know who give them flavored sugar and chocolate covered with a thin candy shell, possibly made of beetle skin. That's not just gross, it's downright bizarre.

So, anyway, America is starting to believe that we might actually BE what we eat. And so we want to eat a little bit healthier but still enjoy our food. It's just a twist, not a full on hokey-pokey turn ourselves around. Business owners know this. They also know how fearfully reactionary we are, especially about our food supply. And thus was born the emerging business of bovine genealogy. We now have people whose job it is to trace the lineage of a cow so that potential steak eaters will know that he, or she, didn't come from plowed over rainforest land or didn't have a wacky "Mad" ancestor. Nobody likes an angry cow.

Munchingtons was a semi-regional steak house chain in Alabama and Mississippi. And, like most restaurants, it suffered in its first year. Granted, that was mainly due to disgruntled customers who expected to be served by midgets, but they eventually came to accept the taller wait-staff and came to love and crave the juicy cow meat loins and flanks. And then there was another Mad Cow Disease scare. The twenty-four hour news cycle can simply kill a restaurant. So, instead of closing up shop or adjusting his menu, owner, Raymond Parke, went in a different direction. He hired famed bovine genealogist, Anne Marie Nathaniel, to meticulously research the origins of each cow he cooked. Besides her field research (some pun intended), Anne printed out human-style ancestry charts for the customers' perusal. The people loved it. It seemed like such a simple solution, and it indeed was. But that doesn't mean that it's an easy job.

Cows tend to live in the moment. You can see it in their zest for life and preference for adventure sports. This makes them fun dates, but it also means that they don't generally know much about their ancestors. And a wise man once said something about not knowing where you're going if you don't know where you've been. I don't think he was talking specifically about heifers, but you never know.

Anyway, Anne Marie was in Kansas trying to track down the parents of Bobby, a Guernsey from Mississippi, who'd seemed a little wobbly when she interviewed him. Bobby couldn't even remember who his parents were or where he had been born. He was adopted, along with a hundred other cows by a kindly gentleman from Chicago who runs a house of some kind. Early cow separation can have long lasting effects on the psyche of a bovine. So, it was Anne Marie's job, nay, her mission, to discover if Bobby's wobbliness was due to some dread disease or simply repressed memories from his own calfhood. After conducting twenty fruitless interviews it occurred to Anne Marie that parents miss their kids, even cow parents. And when Anne Marie circulated a picture of Bobby, his mother came charging up to Anne Marie to discover what had become of her beloved calf. Luckily Anne Marie wasn't wearing red.

After a lengthy conversation, motherhood was officially established. Bobby's mom shared some cute stories of his early years: his first salt lick, his first day of school, that time when Bobby had tried to hump a goat. Ahhh, it was a pleasant afternoon for both women. Bobby's mother was reassured that her son had a good life and was off trying to discover a good cow weight-loss technique, and yet another future Munchington's customer was reassured that he was eating a cow from a good family.

The restaurant business can be tough, but as Calvin Coolidge once said, "The business of America is business." We're great at adjusting to the ever-changing times. If you don't believe me, look up Velcro, the history of automotive mileage standards, or ask Anne Marie Nathaniel, bovine genealogist.

THE ORGAN RECITAL

Sheldon J. Kupfman had always been a planner. He was the four-year-old who told his friends where to hide and then found them. He was the twelve-year-old who meticulously plotted the course of toilet papering during the week leading up to the Friday night raid. He was the sixteen-year-old who picked just the right homeless guy to buy the beer. Sheldon was just one of those guys who saw the plan in his head and then made it happen.

After graduating from his Biotech PhD program, Sheldon made some of the standard somewhat medical rounds: working for the CDC, a stint in hospital administration dealing with the whiners, interning with a stem cell research lab. All of it was interesting, but not as fulfilling as he'd hoped. Finally, Sheldon J. Kupfman wound up in a job he loved, one that incorporated his life-long love of the plan. He was an organ donor traffic cop. He was the guy who decided which organs went where.

Sheldon did his job well. It helps if you love your work. In fact, Sheldon got so good at his duties that his bosses let him expand it and bring it more into the public domain. If you're feeling brave or curious, you too can visit his website and plan out the final destinations of your own internal organs. It's pretty damn fun.

Unfortunately for Sheldon, reality doesn't always factor into the fine art of organ donation. In fact, over the years, he's had to deal with some random requests. Although there are too many to list comprehensively, here are a few of the highlights:

—Mr. Ronald T. Bitterman of Alba, Georgia, wants his intestines to be
     donated to the Boys and Girls Club of Atlanta, which might be OK if

he didn't designate that they had to be used to make "a greener, more natural jump rope".

—Mrs. Kelly Thompson of Heart, Oklahoma, wants her uterus to be used as a prize for getting the ring over the milk bottle in a traveling carnival. She'd prefer, although she's not firm on this point, that it first be gilded.

—Mr. Arthur Fredson of Ithaca, New York, always proud of his nasal ability in life, wants his nostrils to be donated to "stuffed-up bomb-sniffing dogs".

—Mrs. Jennifer Branden of Fort Worth, Texas, wants her "excess stomach-related material" to go to elementary school art programs for use as "anti-obesity art".

In a speech to the National Institute of Health, Kupfman said " . . . and most people mean well. They're ideas are not even remotely realistic, and most seem to think that we're all in the Potatohead family, but they do mean well."

For example:

—Mrs. Candy Whitmer of Portland, Oregon, wants the placenta she'd saved on her mantelpiece for fifty years to be rubbed on food drop pallets dropped in remote mountain regions for our military (personally, that'd make me think twice about eating it, but hey, I've never been trapped in an avalanche).

—Mr. Owen Miller of Kansas City, Kansas, wants to will his entire body to Kansas State Medical School for cadaver use, which wouldn't be all that unusual if he weren't one of a pair of Siamese twins and if his twin brother didn't object and wasn't currently alive.

—Mrs. Iona P. Hendricks of Comment, Georgia, wants to will her breasts to Playboy, which is really funny since she's ninety-seven years old.

—Mr. Jonathan Dellinger of Milwaukee, Wisconsin, wants to will his liver to the state historical archives to be bronzed and made into a monument in honor of the beer that made Milwaukee famous.

—Mrs. Penelope Sinclair of San Francisco, California, wants her mustache, so maligned in life, to be used for Biotech research to combat SFMD, Swarthy Female Mustache Disorder.

—Mrs. Christine V. Linkletter of Lowell, Massachusetts, wants her facial mole to be willed to an aspiring pop singer for use as a beauty mark.

Continuing his speech, Kupfman said, "Yeah, it's a weird job, but I'm making a handful of people in the afterlife happy. Most of them are probably pretty pissed at me."

KYLE'S HOMEMADE SAUSAGE

Everybody who has ever visited New Bainville knows about Kyle's Homemade Sausage. Hell, it's what put the town back on the map. A century ago, New Bainville, then known as Old Bainville, was a thriving center for haberdashery, but alas, those days have long since faded and, nowadays, no one even knows what a haberdasher is. I sure don't. But I know about Kyle's Homemade Sausage. You see, I was an apprentice under Kyle himself three summers ago. I've since left the world of man-made meat products, but I'll never forget that fateful summer.

I arrived at the front office, hat in hand, a young aspiring meat packer, dewy behind the ears, with a kick in my step that only amphetamines could provide. The front door was so intimidating that it took me three tries before I actually worked up the courage to walk inside.

Oh, but once I entered the front door, what a rush it was. People were scurrying past me, some holding animal products, some with strange exciting instruments, others with paper. I may have only had three dollars in my pocket and a knapsack full of dreams, but I knew that sausage was the future. It was part of the past, too, but I thought at the time that it would be big in the future. I was right and I was wrong.

The front desk was manned by a short-statured, gruff-looking man named Phil. Phil directed the sausage tours, took applications from prospective sausateers, and shouted encouraging, vaguely communistic slogans to the workers.

"Keep your chin up, Virgil. Death to the bourgeois."

"Hello, is this where I can apply for a job?"

"Let me look you over, son. What makes you think that you've got what it takes to pack meat?"

"Well, I like meat. I like touching meat and putting it into tubes."

"Good enough. Get thee down to Brenda in Human Resources. It's down the hall and to the left. And remember, one day the proletariat will rise up in revolution."

"Uh, OK."

Human Resources was run by Brenda. She was a stern task mistress who ruled the department with the whip and the fang. Entering the large double doors, I was assaulted by the sounds of ten burly men grunting as they pushed a large wooden wheel around. Brenda was on horseback, riding around the outside of the wheel, shouting "Mush" and occasionally whipping one of the men when they got out of line. Her metallic breastplate shone in the soft 40 watt light.

"Who are you?"

"I'm Steven J. Ironhold. I'm new."

"Are you a eunuch?"

"I'm sorry, a eunuch?"

"Do you have genitalia?"

"Last time I checked."

"Well this is Eunuch Resources. You want Human Resources. It's next door."

"Are you Brenda?"

"Yeah, go next door and I'll be there in a minute . . . mush eunuchs, push harder, dickless ones."

The Human Resources room was much more comforting and a lot less medieval. There were comfortable, cushioned chairs which smelled vaguely of syrup lining the walls. There was a coffee machine. There were men in suits and women in pantsuits. There were Rollos available at the touch of a button. It was pleasant.

After five minutes of simply enjoying the pleasing pleasantness of this room, I felt pleased. Brenda entered through a crawl space that connects the two rooms. She had changed into an appealing gray skirt and a white button-down shirt.

"Steven?"

"Yes, ma'am."

"Follow me. You are to be tested."

I followed Brenda down the hall, past the water cooler and the desks, through the large glass doors that separate the Waiting Room from the Doing Room. The Doing Room was eerie. There was one fourth-grade-style desk in the middle of the room, with the metal seat and the wooden folding top that conceals whatever may lie inside.

"The first test is of your psychic abilities."

"Brenda, you know that I'm here to learn about sausage, right?"

"Of course. Now tell me, what is inside that desk."

I concentrated, summoning all of the Zen energy that my guru/third grade teacher, Miss Hendrickson, had taught me. Finally, it came to me in a flash.

"Inside is the sound of one hand clapping."

"Actually it's sausage. Most people get that one. Moving on. Tell me, what are the three principles of sausage construction?"

"Number one, don't think about it. Number two, spicy mustard destroys the brain cells that would allow the eater to be disgusted by the fact that he just ate rat hair. And three, oh darn it to heck, what's three? I can't remember."

"Two out of three, not bad. For the record, the third principle of sausagation is to set your inner sausage free. It's easier said than done. OK, well, you did alright on your first two tests, but now comes the third and final test. Close your eyes. Hold out your hands. I'm going to put this lump of meat byproducts in your left hand and this packaging in your right hand. You have two minutes to make a sausage."

"Without looking at it?"

"Trust your feelings. Be the sausage."

I did it. It wasn't a perfectly straight, round cylinder like Kyle makes, but it was good enough to get me the job. Oh, what a happy day that was. I ran home yelling, "I'm a sausage maker. I'm going to make sausages." En route I saw Old Man Richter, who tousled my hair, gave me some hard candy and six shillings, and wished me the best of luck in my new endeavor.

I'm not going to lie to you. The first few weeks were tough. I had to be up at the crack of dawn and at the plant, geared up and ready to go before the rooster crowed. I hated that damn bird. Later, the rooster met his fate and became part of sausage lore forever when he won the cock fight at the Fourteenth Annual Sausagefest, the annual celebration of all things sausage. Those were glorious celebrations. There were men getting dunked into vats of sausage, men slurping sausage smoothies, men dressed as sausages, men sword fighting with sausage links, men throwing sausage patties for distance. Ahh, the Sausagefest, not a lot of women, but fun.

I can vividly remember my first day on "the floor". I was sweeping up discarded goat entrails when I saw Tim Guster. My Lord, it was Tim Guster in the flesh. He's as big a sausage legend as they come, next to Kyle himself, of course. It's rumored that Tim Guster, about to miss a large order in the near meat shortage of '68, actually cross-bred a rat and a griffin to make the first riffin, now a staple of all Kyle's sausages. The legend says that Tim was able to verbally convince all the riffins that sacrificing themselves to the sausage gods was the only way for them to avoid being deported back to Romania. Granted, riffins aren't known for their intelligence, but they do make good sausage.

Tim saw me staring at him in awe, and, being a consummate gentleman, came over and introduced himself. It was like meeting the Pope or Elvis. He even signed my Sausage Card (and it was his rookie card). He gave me some sau-sage advice which I'll never forget:

"Son, what I've learned over the years can be summed up in one sentence. Always wash your hands."

"Wow, th, thank, you, sir."

"Now get back to work. Those cat livers won't mash themselves into a fine paste."

"Yes, sir."

But the day I treasure most was the day that I met the man himself, Kyle. When he wasn't touring the country on his Sausage Lecture Series, Kyle spent most of his time in the board room making high-level decisions and deciding the future of sausage. It was April. April third, a Tuesday. It was 1:47 in the P.M. I had just finished mixing a pound of East Asian dog tongues into the vat marked "?" when I saw him. Light preceded him. Light followed him wherever he went. He shined. He shimmered. He was a sausage deity. Looking tired, but regal, Kyle walked out of the board room, which was located on the second level of the building, just above "the floor". We could all see people coming and going from the board room, but it was like looking at a different world. We may have made the sausages, but the people on the second level, they lived, ate, slept and breathed sausage. Well, most of them didn't eat it, but the rest is true.

Kyle walked out of the board room and up to the railing. He surveyed his kingdom, all the little workers playing their parts. We were wheels in a cog, or maybe cogs in a wheel, yeah, cogs in a wheel. I saw Kyle look directly at me as I was stirring the "?" vat with the huge wooden spoon, occasionally stopping to taste heaven. Then the strangest thing happened. He smiled, at me. Kyle smiled at me. He winked an encouraging "Keep Up the Good Work, you Little Scamp" wink. I felt alive for the first time ever.

At first I had been placed under Yambo, the meat wizard, to learn the art of differentiating types of meat. Yambo was a genius. Everybody knew it. He could taste a meat and tell you not only what animal it came from, but what part of the animal, where the animal was from, and what the animal had itself eaten before it was killed and gutted. On his good days, which were few because of his weekly heart attacks, Yambo could simply smell a piece of meat and tell you everything about it. I learned a lot from Yambo. It was sad the day that I found him dead, slumped over the grinder, a piece of South American squirrel haunch inches away from his nose. I don't know what happened to Yambo's body, but the moment of silence we all observed for him was a beautiful thing. We were all tearing up and sniffling, even Irene who we thought had lost the ability to smell or to cry from extended exposure to ammonia (she lived in a house made of ammonia).

Those were the happy days, the meat salad days if you will. Soon I began to notice things, strange things, upsetting things. It was a Friday. We were all mentally preparing ourselves for the weekend, thinking of ways to spend our paychecks, and dreaming of places where the walls weren't lined with dead animal carcasses. I saw Tim emerge from the Men's Room. He was wiping away tears and snot. I asked him what was wrong, but he couldn't even talk to me. He just ran away, sobbing. Putting it out of my mind, I finished my work day and started heading home. After a dinner of squash soufflé, artichoke, and sausage, I remembered that I'd left my lucky bracelet back at the plant. Well, I'd been working there long enough to have a key, so I just went about heading back to the plant to retrieve my bracelet. I recall that it was raining, hard.

Thunder crackled and lightning whizzed overhead, warning us that the rain was not going to stop any time soon. Entering the plant, I saw Tim Guster and the great Kyle hurriedly pushing something in the grinder. When they saw me, Tim stepped in front of the grinder, and Kyle came over to talk to me.

"Heya, Steven. What're you doing back here?"

He knew my name (of course I was wearing a name tag, but that didn't register at the time).

"Oh, nothing, sir. I left my lucky bracelet in my locker."

"That's right, no arm jewelry on the floor. We wouldn't want some nice lady to find a Seiko in her patty."

"No, sir. We sure wouldn't. Oh, sir, I didn't know that you worked down here on "the floor" late at night. That makes me feel all gooey-good inside."

"Well, what can I say? I love my job."

"What're you two using over there? Is it the spare hamster colons, the deer hooves, what?"

"No, son. This is for a special batch. Shh, it's a secret."

"My lips are sealed, sir."

And then I walked to the locker room to retrieve my bracelet. I was on my way back out when I heard Tim and Kyle whispering.

"You think he suspects anything?"

"No, let's lock up and go to Joe's. We'll meet back here in the morning and finish up."

Were they talking about me? They must've thought that I'd left, since they locked the doors. Letting my curiosity get the better of me, I had to go and check out the work of the master. I wish to God that I hadn't. But I did. Approaching the grinder I saw a size ten and a half Reebok sticking out. It's a human leg.

Kyle's homemade sausage is people. It's people.

MARQUEE MADNESS, part two

Technically, Thomas was still a marquee consultant. That's what it said on his business card. But, having narrowly survived the mob attack on his life in Gainesville, GA, Thomas was more hesitant in his job, more restrained, more cautious. Also, he no longer works for penis doctors.

Still, Thomas needed to pay his rent, and he'd basically already cornered the marqueet, since no else in the country even has his job. In other words, Thomas still does what he does, but now it's a little different. Now, he's mad at the world. As you might imagine, it was his Gainesville lynch-mob experience that changed him. With his handy giant translucent-letter bag in tow, Thomas now has the equivalent of a second career as a Super Criminal. Thomas is the world's only non-pre-teen Marquee Terrorist.

During the day, Thomas is still a mild-mannered consultant, but at night he puts on black spandex and a ski mask and becomes the irritating sore on the butt of the Detroit business community. Also his manners get less mild.

Despite his desire to create marquee havoc, Thomas still is a businessman at heart. So, he never terrorizes his own work, and, in fact, uses his nightly activities as an effective method of garnering more business. For example:

The Burger Den's sign used to read: "Monday Special—Free Shake With Burger" and Thomas changed that to "Mommy Special: Free Mammogram With Burger"—the next day the Burger Den called Thomas. But Jose' and George, the fry cooks, enjoyed giving those first two breast exams.

The Hair Silo's sign read: "Highlights, Frosting, Dye Jobs, We Do It All"—Thomas changed that to: 'Now Herpes Free, We Do It All'—the next day he got a call.

City Hall's Voter Registration Drive sign read: "Register by Mid-Summer and Feel Patriotic"—Thomas changed it too: "Kiss your local representative . . . with tongue"—predictably, Thomas got a new gig the next day, coinciding with the inevitable lawsuit.

Kelly's Drive-Thru Massage Parlor (which, due to the inherent ridiculousness of her store, really needed a good marketing campaign) had a sign that read: "Put it in Park, Lay Back, and Let Me Touch You", which is disturbing enough as is—but after Thomas got through with it, it became "Put it in Park, Lay Back, and Pay Me To Touch You"—Kelly would've called Thomas the next day, but got arrested before she could (ironically, in the women's lock up her slogan remained "Lay Back and Let Me Touch You", but she was rarely paid for her services).

Orlando's Seeing Eye People, already a slightly sketchy venture, had a largely unnecessary marquee which read: "Man's New Best Friend: Helpful Dwarves". Thomas changed it to: "Handicapped People Are Losers, Let's Hunt Them Down and Steal Their Orthopedic Shoes". Thomas never received the call he'd expected, but that was probably due to the fact that most blind people can't read marquees.

Yes, Thomas was determined to live out his dream. He wouldn't let his near-death experience in Southern vigilante justice stop him. He wouldn't even let the fact that his job is as unnecessary as door-to-door IUD salesman in Vatican City get him down. Thomas was a Marquee Consultant and we love him for that.

THE ONGOING ADVENTURES OF . . . part eight

THE ONGOING ADVENTURES OF THE HAIRLESS PIRATE

Nobody took Cecil Wharton seriously when he boarded their ship and demanded their cargo. That's because he was beardless, and no one's afraid of a beardless pirate.

THE ONGOING ADVENTURES OF THE SARCASTIC SOLDIER

Tyrone Sanderson had been an Army man his entire life. It's what he was destined to do. But, Tyrone had one of those voices/speech patterns that just came off as sarcasm. It wasn't his fault, but sarcasm doesn't play well in the military.

THE ONGOING ADVENTURES OF THE PREPUBESCENT CONGRESSMAN

Amber Luthergaard, the teenage girl Representative from North Dakota, needed to fund-raise for her next campaign. But, the traditional big money men in North Dakota wouldn't take her calls, neither of them. Instead, Amber raised money the old fashioned way—she stole it from her mother's purse. "Paid for by Amber's Mother, sorry mom" came on at the end of every commercial. Americans For Belly Ring Acceptance also gave big to Amber's campaign.

A NEW IDEA

American politics is something to watch. Even if it is all a rigged money game, it's still combative and interesting enough to make you pay attention. They say that the one constant in life, and I think Todd Bridges will back me up on this, is that things change. And politics changes with the times. Some political candidates just throw who they are out there and see if it sticks. Others comb over polling data and create a persona, and that's what runs for office. Roger Irving was one of those people.

Unlike many of his predecessors, Roger didn't lean on political polling data. But he was a trend-watcher. Noticing that more people vote for American Idol than in a presidential election, Roger decided to give the people what they want in an elected leader. Above all else, Roger Irving wanted to be electable. And, as far as I know, he was the first person to ever run for the Mississippi state senate based partially on his cool dance moves.

Roger's sister, Melinda, had worked as a reality show developer for one of the TV networks. And, as the older sister, Melinda always felt compelled to tell her little brother what to do and how to do it. Just because her little brother was in his fifties and had six kids himself doesn't mean that sibling roles change that much. It was this kind of thinking that led Roger Irving to go back and study break dancing tapes for his first fundraiser.

Since his campaign was based on reality TV, Roger, upon announcing his candidacy, hired Erik Estrada to introduce him at all his campaign stops. Apparently, it's a rule that reality TV needs an out-of-work B-level, former TV star as a host. Roger's constituents might have accepted his campaign strategy more easily if he'd stopped the reality show tie-ins there. They were a bit puzzled with the direction his campaign was taking, however, even the crustiest old statesman had to admit that adding an "I'll-eat-whatever-you-dare-me-to-for-your-vote" aspect to his stump speech did bring in the crowds. And after you've eaten ten used Band-aids, a French-to-English dictionary, seven lawn ornaments and a box of Lego's, your stomach can handle pretty much anything. Making his audiences jump through razor-sharp hula hoops of fire was original. Getting the entire cast of "Saved by the Bell" to join him on stage was a work of genius. Think about it, no matter what your political leanings, if you had a Hollywood crush on a TV idol in your formative years, you're going to show up and see him or her, even if only to reassure you that getting married was the right idea or to remind yourself that those five years you spent in the bushes across from Kelly Kapowski's house weren't wasted.

Roger also managed to inspire the masses with cardboard, a feat not accomplished since the glory days of Turbo. And Roger briefly caught the nation's attention with his "Bungee-Jump-for-Tort-Reform" stunt.

Roger enjoyed the polling bump he got when he lived with four aging rock stars/former drug addicts in their posh Malibu home. Making out with Joan Jett didn't hurt him in the red portion of Mississippi (pretty much all of it except that one gay couple's house in Jackson).

Sure, Roger Irving lost the election, and by a landslide, but it was fun to watch.

ORIGINALITY

The origins of things (ideas, inventions, what not) are often forgotten, or, more often than that, the origins of things get muddled in that weird little mish-mash of truth, innuendo, and propaganda that we call "history". That's the way it is, the way it was, and probably the way it will be until the robots take over and make us slaves working in their paprika mines in the year 2018.

Rico Thompson was an originalist: (Am, 21st cen.) 1-one who studies the origins of whatever, 2-one who cannot find gainful employment.

Rico was giving a speech to the bright young scamps of Sunnydawn Middle School in MintMilano, Mississippi (they never got the sponsorship funding they wanted and now the city council wishes that it had gone with its original name idea of Ringdingington). There were to be questions and, hopefully, answers.

" . . . and so it was actually not Thomas Crapper, but a feisty British nobleman named John Harrington who invented the indoor flush toilet, and yet we still use the word 'crap' and not something more along the lines of 'I've got to take a Harrington'. But some old folks like me still use the term 'John' which we can assume to be derived from Harrington's first name. Any toilet-related questions?"

"Any toilet-related questions?" has been scientifically proven to be the worst question to ask to an assembled group of junior high schoolers, narrowly beating out "So, who here masturbates?"

"Um, Mr. Thompson, I've got a toilet-related question. Why is doo-doo brown?"

It got some laughs, but it was a good question. Rico went with the standard, "brown is the combination of all colors" line. It was enough to satisfy the inquiring minds of the audience, but not enough to stop the barrage of doo-doo related questions which followed. It took Rico twenty minutes before he could transition the perverse audience out of bodily-function territory. The highlights included:

Why is some doo-doo runny?

Why does it curl around like a turban in the toilet?

Why does it burn when I pee (that kid didn't realize that at his thirty year reunion people would still remember his junior high question and continue to make fun of him for being the youngest kid in Chattahoosa County to ever contract Chlamydia)?

Why isn't doo-doo more solid so that I could play with it?

Why is baby poo green?

And there were many, many more.

Finally Rico got them to segue up the colon and into the stomach—food territory.

"Is Jell-O really made from horse hooves?"

"Good question. I believe that it's mainly synthetic now, but yeah at first it was all horse. I don't know the first person to think of that, but what a moment that must've been—some guy was just absentmindedly chopping off horse's feet, whistling a happy work tune, and he runs out of trail mix, so then he decides to melt down a hoof and eat it. What a strange world we live in. Can you imagine how he got the next guy to eat it? No come on, yeah it's a hoof, but just try it. But that's the thing, most of the biggest discoveries were accidents—penicillin, Jell-O, this country, you name it."

"What about the Internet? Did Al Gore really invent the Internet?"

"No, but he was one of the original Senate sponsors who thought to make this military program available to the public."

"Was Las Vegas really founded by the mob?"—"Yes".

"Why is the sky blue?"—"Shortest wavelength in the color spectrum, so more easily scattered."

"Why do you look so creepy?"—"I'm wearing an ascot."

"Why is TV so bad?"—"Simple market forces, in other words, you kids have bad taste."

"Are you better off being vegetarian?"—"Maybe, Ben Franklin, Plato, Voltaire, all went veg, at least for a while. They said yes. And yeah, there really are growth hormones in most US beef. But, if you stop eating meat there's a good chance that you'll become a transvestite."—"Really?"—"No, just seeing if you were still paying attention."

And those were just some excerpts from Rico Thompson's junior high speech/Q & A session. After the talk he promptly had his tubes tied.

ONE STOP SHOPPING

Paulie and Shirley McFadden were one of those couples who does everything together. You see these couples out at the mall or at the park—they're the ones in matching outfits who finish each other's sentences and wipe mustard off of each other's cheeks when appropriate. They're cute. They're in vogue. They make you want to vomit.

Paulie had grown up in a retail family. His dad was one of the last successful door-to-door buffalo salesmen. His mother started her own business sewing discarded mittens together to make really big mittens for people with unusually large hands. Shirley's father and mother were both managers at a Woolworth's, the pre-Target, Target.

Together the McFaddens were a capitalistic force to be reckoned with. Although their first few business ventures were unsuccessful (no one wanted their Tofu Stuffed Animals and the drive-through fertilizer store, while original, didn't provide employees with the most sterile work environment). But adversity didn't stop the McFaddens.

One afternoon, Paulie and Shirley sat down at John Ridge Park and plotted their next move. They batted around ideas for a prenatal toy store, but then figured that pregnant women would have a hard time getting the toys to the embryos. They discussed the lack of rodent-themed restaurants. Finally, they saw a woman walk by carrying a full bag from one of those discount everything stores, like Woolworth's only bigger, more profitable, and so powerful that the author doesn't want to get sued so he won't even mention the name. But it starts with a W and ends with an almart.

That's when inspiration struck Paulie McFadden. He realized what the world needs is another humongous superstore. His wife mentioned that perhaps America had reached its saturation point with regard to the Mega everything'sforsalesuperstores. But then Paulie added a new twist. "Sure," he said, "we've got superstores that sell every product under the sun, but

I'm talking about a true, honest to God, everything store, where you can not only buy everything you need, but also get whatever else you need. Not just products, other areas of life."

And that was the glorious beginning of Everyfreakingthings, the super chain that's now so popular that I hardly even need to mention it. You've been there. We've all been there. There's one in every town, sometimes two or three. And Everyfreakingthings truly has every freaking thing. Not only is there an expansive, but not expensive, grocery store, there's also an electronics department, a clothing department for men, women, boys and girls, a furniture department, an auto parts department, a proctology department (no cameras there), a home furnishings department, a pharmaceutical department, a book store, a movie rental store for the elderly who can't operate Netflicks, a barber, an optometrist, a specialty/ethnic foods department, an allergist, an on-call dentist, an athletic supply department, and a food court. But every large chain discount store has those departments nowadays. That's not what makes Everyfreakingthings special.

They also have a Romance Department. Why not? It's something that we're all searching for, and those matchmaker services have pretty well proven that we're willing to pay for a long shot at love. Capitalizing on that unfortunate trend, the McFaddens created the Romance Department, which, over Paulie's objection, is not a euphemism for a brothel. Instead, the McFaddens hired various non-sexual prostitutes to work as "dates" for lonely, lonely men. Sex is not part of the bargain (although if the employee should work something out on her own, well, let's just say that she probably won't have to pay taxes on it). For a while they hired a few men to act as dates for lonely women, but, it turns out that most women found the prospect rather creepy and the men were quickly transferred to the stock room, where they are free to talk about sex with customers, and often do, but are discouraged from acting on said impulses.

One of the most popular areas of the stores is the Self-Esteem Department. At first, Paulie failed to see the business sense in a department which sells absolutely nothing, but, after only a few weeks, Shirley had convinced her husband that this is good for business, really good for business. The Self-Esteem Department is designed as a simple gauntlet. Position #1 is for fashion commentary. Position #2 is for physical beauty commentary. And Position #3 is for randomly complimentary commentary. Basically the customer walks through the one long hallway pausing at the three prearranged stops. At the first stop a professional fashion commentator gives the customer a compliment about his or her clothes. "Hey, nice tie," "Are those some snazzy dungarees or what?" and "That halter top is so cute, I just want to rip your head off and steal it," are just some of the sample compliments that the handbook suggests. Prospective hirees for Position #2 need to be born ass-kissers to be effective. Some people are just born rump lickers, and those folks do well in Everyfreakingthings Self-Esteem Department. "Are those your abs or are you wearing a muscle suit?", "Dear God you've got a sexy widow's peak," and "Your chin makes me want to suck on it for about an hour," are, again, just a few of the sample compliments. Position #3 is for free—flowing compliments. It doesn't matter what the Position 3ers say, as long as it's taken as a compliment by the customer. Shirley was right—this is a good idea. People leave the Self-Esteem Department feeling like they could take on the world, bank account minimum balance be damned.

But the Self-Esteem Department isn't even the most shockingly original aspect of the McFaddens' dream store. They have recently added a Spirituality Department in order to address the growing supernatural void that accompanies 21st century American life. For the true searcher who doesn't have the money to visit the Holy Land, sit at the feet of the Buddha, or buy enough oranges (or whatever) to find the one with the image of the Virgin Mary inside, there's the Spirituality Department. The department is based on the commonly held, but weird, idea that wise men sit on top of mountains, that they all have long white, slightly unkempt, beards, and that they're willing to share some of their wisdom with you if you survive the dangerous trek up the mountain. Unfortunately, the McFaddens had neither the space nor the insurance to install actual mountains. Instead, they hired a bunch of unemployed Guatemalans to act as sherpas. Americans don't know the difference between a Tibetan and a Central American anyway, and, thanks to Richard Gere, Tibetans cost too much. Upon entering the Spirituality Department, a fake sherpa doses you with LSD and then, after a thirty minute fast-motion lecture while the drug works its way in, customers are led into the "Mountain Room", which, as you know, doesn't contain an actual mountain. Luckily, most non-experienced drug users don't know this. And once they've traversed the escalator and talked to the skinny, old man with the fake beard—once he's read them some pithy piece of advice he found on a Bazooka Joe wrapper—then they seem to feel somehow fuller, more satisfied. Next, the customer is led into the swirling colors room where there's plenty of water and plenty of 2-6 year-old age inappropriate toys to play with. Finally, after a nine hour ordeal, the newly Zen customer is let out of the Spirituality Department through a door that opens onto the Food Court. This was another brilliant idea. After a nine hour drug trip, curly fries and milkshakes sound like manna from heaven, which was the idea to begin with.

The Everyfreakingthing store is only the latest in one stop shopping experiences. It will someday be surpassed by another chain offering automotive massage or scalpel—free vasectomies, but not yet. For now, the McFaddens dream is a profitable reality. May you live in interesting times.

DIFFICULT ARGUMENTS THROUGHOUT HISTORY

Hello, I'm Kendall "the Aardvark" Aardson, host of *Difficult Arguments Throughout History*. Since it's the end of the year, we here at DATH thought that it might be nice to have an end-of-the-year, best-of kind of show. We know you've all been waiting the whole year for this, so here goes:

"No sir, Mister Congressman, I don't think that it's in any way inhumane to club baby seals. In fact, they love it. It's like a game to them, sir. I'm sorry, what was that? Oh, well, sure sometimes it takes four or five whacks to kill them, but that's all part of the fun of clubbing baby seals."

"No, doctor, I just don't agree with you. I mean, think about it, doc. Crack babies are born with so much added energy that most of them learn to walk well before their peers. And, honestly, who wants a fat baby?"

"I think you're right, America **is** ready for a transvestite evening news anchor."

"I know you're the editor, but I just don't think that Muslims take that Mohammed guy all that seriously. We can lampoon him. A picture of their prophet in a yarmulke, that's not going to make anybody mad. The cartoon of him playing hopscotch with Jesus and Buddha, no it's cute, and besides, if Muslims are known for anything, it's their sense of humor."

"No Mr. Nader, I think America is ready for a president who's so unbelievably boring that he makes John Kerry look almost lifelike."

"Declare war on Antarctica . . . why not?"

"No, Lee, it's easy. All you have to do is go sit by the window in that book depository with this high-powered rifle."

"Well, if you say that it's just Kool-Aid, Mr. Jones, then that's good enough for me."

"My fellow advertising executives, don't worry, the black community is going to love our cute, little syrup mascot. Really, how could anyone take offense at an obese black mamie hawking syrup in the twentieth century?"

"But who's going to buy clothes from a homosexual designer?"

"You've never even tried yodeling, Mr. Sinatra, how do you know that no one wants to hear it?"

"Well, sure, I'll sleep with you, Wilt. Wait, you're not going to tell anybody, are you?"
"Well, you are a uniter, Governor Bush, might as well say it."

"So what if it is on TV, Mr. Nixon, you're every bit as handsome as that Kennedy guy."

"It looks just like natural hair, Mr. Trump."

"Trail of Tears? No, my Cherokee brother, it's going to be a Trail of Giggles."

"No, he's not getting blown. She's just tying his shoes under the desk. He just really enjoys getting his shoes tied."

"I'm telling you, Genghis, forget this whole conquer-the-world thing, history remembers yak herders."

"Sure we're still fighting the Americans, but with the housing market in Hiroshima like it is, we'd be stupid *not* to move there."

"Unprotected anal sex with you? Well, I guess it's all part of the jail experience."

"Don't worry, Czarina, nobody's ever going to find out about you and this cow."

"You're new to Ellis Island, I see. Your name is Gunther Czarinickszisternhandelson. Let's rename you . . . Bob Smith."

"Just let them Nazis in. Nobody's going to remember this and, for sure, no one will ever make fun of Poland."

"Don't worry about a condom, dude. It's proven fact that no Vietnamese women have venereal diseases."

RED, WHITE AND BLOWN AWAY

It all happened so slowly that few people could truly see the big picture. At first it was just the little things, but gradually we accomplished our barely hidden goal of making the rest of the world less scary. In other words we've turned the entire world into suburban Kansas City.

Very few sociologists pointed out the irony that America, the birthplace of tobacco, had become the most virulently anti-tobacco country in the world. Public service campaigns, not being able to smoke in the hospital, warning labels, the symbolic firing squad killing of the once-beloved phallic children's icon, Joe Camel—all of these things were representative of the U.S.'s new anti-smoking stance. And the rest of the world, wanting our tourist dollars, quickly followed suit.

I like the way the Japanese did it. Everybody in Japan smokes, so, using their famous Hondagenuity, Japan designed the first non-smoking, smoking restaurant in the known world. It's simple: two pneumatic tubes descend from the ceiling above your table, post meal—one with a pre-lit cigarette in it, the other for smoke exhalation. Once exhaled, the smoke is then pumped out and released above the restaurant where no one who's not ten feet tall can breathe it, effectively protecting everyone in Japan except Mothra. You can smoke after a meal without having the Japanese PTA mom complain about second-hand smoke. This development was weird, no doubt, but effective. RJR Reynolds executives were so appreciative that they declared the invention day a Japanese national holiday. No one in Japan noticed.

The Amber alert system was adopted in Thailand. You know what I'm talking about—the electronic screens telling the name and physical description of the kidnapped child so that motorists can be on the lookout for bad guys when they're pumping gas at the Citgo. Well, Thailand has a lot of kidnappings, so they tried to import this system, but, without the funds for the technology, they have more of a Tran-alert system. Tran is the name of the guy the government hired to stand up high and look for kidnappings. He hasn't found any yet, but at least his mother is proud of him now.

By far the strangest recent American trend export has to be our prescription drug commercials on TV thing. This is an awful, awful trend in any country, but some of the sub-Saharan African prescription drug commercials are pretty funny. "Ask your witch doctor if N'Toula's Shrunken Heads are right for you—may cause demonic possession, ancestral shame, and Ebola."

We used to export good stuff: soy beans, corn, wood pulp, cars, airplanes . . . raw materials, technology. Now we give the world eerie social trends and drugged-out pop singers. God Bless America!!

THE FUTURE OF DAY CARE

Let's face it, young mothers run this country. If you look at it from a "hand that rocks the cradle" standpoint, they always have. However, nowadays, they just straight up determine the direction of the country. If it was truly still a man's country, then alimony would be a something that divorced guys laugh about in sports bars and not what they cry about in sports bars. If it was truly still a man's country, then the age of consent wouldn't be eighteen. And then there's the most obvious, and annoying, piece of evidence that, despite what your hippie-ass Woman's Studies Major cousin at Bryn-Mahr says, it *is* a woman's country—people bring their kids everywhere.

OK, first off, it's just an annoying trend. Fifty years ago they would have run you out of the hotel restaurant if you'd brought screaming kids in with you to dine, or, at least, you'd feel appropriately embarrassed about it and flee with your head hung down in shame. Nowadays, the screaming little ones are everywhere. You can complain about it, but no one cares.

Robert Massengill saw this trend and, being an entrepreneurial kind of guy, saw the financial potential. Robert was one of those guys who managed to make money trading baseball cards when he was a kid. He sold weed in high school. He sold test answers in college. He sold speed in business school. And after receiving his MBA, from prison since he was technically a drug dealer, he branched out. The first thing Robert did upon release was take his girl, Patty, out to one of those suburban chain restaurants. While enjoying his puffy rolls and fresh Cuyahoga trout, his idyllic meal was interrupted by two screaming babies from three tables over. As he and Patty were shooting knowing "annoyance loves company" looks at the other non-baby-having tables, inspiration struck Robert. Much like his wise decision to stop using toilet paper in prison as means of protecting his last bastion of virginity, Robert's new epiphany was a grand one which would yield positive results. If young families are going to drag their little brats out everywhere anyway, then why not set up day care facilities everywhere? That way parents can still monitor their little ones and the adults can act like adults, instead of having to say things like "fudge", "son of a bee" and the always popular "Shiiioooott" (for when you've started your cuss and then realize in mid-word that an enraptured five-year-old is sitting next to you).

Robert was a whirlwind kind of guy—one of those gets-an-idea-in-his-head-and—everything-else-fades-to-black-while-he-zealously-pursues-his-goal kind of guys. And so, when Robert started We Care (llc.), it took off like a rocket. Robert concentrated on the obvious—the places where everyone pretty much agrees that Day Care is long overdue, restaurants. And once "USA Today" did a piece on his first few successful day care additions to restaurants, Robert got more business than he could handle. In fact, Robert's We Care (llc.) was so successful that it spawned a few imitators. Day Careful, Kiddie Care, and Children Matter were the three non-insane copycats of Robert's original vision. But it was Fredrick Herman's Kid Box that really makes this a story.

Fredrick Herman was Robert's cellmate in prison. And, unlike Robert, Fredrick wasn't what you'd call a visionary. Well, that's not true. He did have visions, but that was mainly because he was a crack head. During their shared time in the clink, Fredrick became a bit of a follower of Robert. He liked Robert's energy, enthusiasm, and non-raping. When Robert shaved his head to look tough, so did Fredrick. When Robert converted to Confucianism in jail, so did Fredrick. And so, once Fredrick had paid his debt to society and was re-released into the wild, he set about copying Robert Massengill once again.

Robert started adding day care centers to restaurants. Fredrick liked the idea, but the restaurant thing had already been done. Fredrick needed some new places. First, he tried brothels. Most of the big Nevada ranches already had day care, so Fredrick concentrated on other states. Unfortunately, prostitution is illegal in other states. When will we ever learn? And, once seven toddlers were busted for playing with blocks, while their mothers were playing with Lincoln Logs, Fredrick took the hint and moved on.

Fredrick's next day care idea was firing ranges, but some states are fussy about letting children frolic in buildings designed for gun play, so that didn't really pan out. The Better Business Bureau, the one which existed in Fredrick's mind, suggested adding day care to doctors' offices.

The children's toy possibilities at the proctologist's office alone seemed like reason enough to do this, but, despite being rich, doctors are some of the worst capitalists on the planet. Even still, Fredrick couldn't find a doctor insane and desperate enough to let a drug-addled crazy person set up a child care facility at his office.

Fredrick expanded his possibilities. Truck stop day care would've worked, but even crazy people try to avoid truck stops, as do young mothers. His condom factory day care idea was just a little too ironic and bad for business. And, after being rejected by NASA for his MIRcare idea (if you can learn to crawl in zero gravity, Earth is a piece of cake), Fredrick turned back to his trusty first business enterprise of selling squirrels to badgers. It's not very lucrative, but the badgers sure are appreciative.

THE ONGOING ADVENTURES OF . . . part nine

THE ONGOING ADVENTURES OF THE
MELLOW SPORTSCASTER

It's pretty much a given that if you want to be on TV, you need to be energetic, or at least not stoned all the time. Roberto Matos never understood that idiom. You might be able to get away with being mellow as a news anchor, or maybe even as a weather man if you're funny or interesting in some wacky way. But you simply can't be an unexcitable sportscaster. You also should try and avoid talking about how much you love Otter Pops in the middle of a sportscast.

THE ONGOING ADVENTURES OF THE
TED NUGENT BOOK CLUB

It was a small, but dedicated, group. No one understood why Ted Nugent, one—time guitar player, turned celebrity death spokesman, would start a book club. It was a fairly natural transition for Oprah Winfrey, but less so for Ted Nugent. And the world was even more surprised when it realized that all of Ted's recommendations were about gay sex under water. Still, *Jennie Has Two Daddies Who Both Get The Bends* is better than you'd think. And, *What Happens In the Marianas Trench, Stays in the Marianas Trench* is some damn impressive prose.

THE ONGOING ADVENTURES OF THE
PREPUBESCENT CONGRESSWOMAN

Amber Luthergaard (D-North Dakota) had been a fixture in the halls of Congress for over a year now. The distinguished gentlegirl was adjusting.

She was a little disappointed when she discovered that the National Mall didn't have a Gap. She did love it that her Secret Service detail only let cute boys within her perimeter. And she soon discovered that high school gossip can't hold a candle to the rumor-mill that is our legislative branch. Her Spin-The-Bottle suggestion for the cloak room went over really well.

THE ONGOING ADVENTURES OF THE WRITER WHO CAN'T THINK OF ANY NEW ONGOING ADVENTURES

Bowen Craig was a writer, but not necessarily a good one. Still, he wrote a lot and hadn't yet found sponsorship for his semi-professional co-ed naked earthworm hunting team, so he was earning his living writing. However, Bowen was currently having a hard time thinking of anything remotely original to add to his Ongoing Adventures Of . . . series. He briefly considered writing those Sesame Street spelling characters who bring the first half of the word together to meet the second half and what would happen to them if they had rapid onset dyslexia or a quick bout of Turret's Syndrome and wound up spelling only really dirty sex words, but then he thought better of it. After that, Bowen thought of a car which runs on sarcasm, but it's not easy showing sarcasm in print, plus his obsession with sarcasm in weird locations was starting to border on the ridiculous. Also it was a bad idea. So, he settled on this stupid and cliché' little-erary trick. Write about how you can't think of anything to write about . . . and consider attending truck driving school.

ST. PRANKSTER

Fred Gaginot had always been a religious man, one of those guys who let his religion dictate everything in his life, a true believer who tried to live according to certain principles. He regularly attended church services. He said a prayer before every meal, even snacks. He even took time to ponder the mysteries of the universe and what role a higher power might play. Granted, that was mainly because he had a two-hour commute to work and a broken radio, but so what? Fred had lived a positive, if rather mundane, life, and firmly believed that he was prepared for any post-mortem contingency. And, since Fred was lost in metaphysical thought while zipping down the highway, he never saw the chicken truck. The next thing he knew, Fred was standing on a cloud with fifteen mangled chickens and three-quarters of a steering wheel in his hand. It suddenly dawned on Fred that he wasn't prepared for this at all.

After a few minutes wait, while Fred and his new poultry buddies were taking stock of the scene, St. Peter appeared. Of course it was St. Peter. Not only was he the guy Fred had expected to be guarding the gate, but he was wearing a nametag.

"What's up, Fred?"

"Uh, um, nothing."

"So, you're dead. You get that, right?"

"Yeah, I figured. Did I do this to these chickens?"

"You did indeed, Fred, and personally, I don't look kindly on chicken manglers, but the Big Guy's got a thing for hot wings, so I guess you won't be reincarnated as an egg. Personally, I've always liked the whole poetic justice thing, but it works better on Asians. So, Fred, any questions?"

"Thousands."

"Heh, I know, but I'm not entirely sure if you're worthy of the answers. Let's find out, shall we?"

"What do you mean, St, uh, Mr. Peter, sir?"

"Have you ever heard of a Life Review, Fred?"

"Like a resume?"

"Kind of like a cosmic resume, yeah. Good analogy. We're going to do one, but first, let me do the chickens' review."

Fred waited while St. Peter apparently let the chickens see their lives. These must've been some sinful chickens since it took a half an hour, during which time Fred paced in front of the gates, which were actually more of a light brown rather than pearly. Finally, St. Peter appeared once again in front of Fred.

"Are the chickens going to heaven?"

St. Peter laughed so hard that he coughed something gross, yet holy, across the cloud.

"No, dude. I was kidding. For the most part chickens don't disobey God's commandments. I'm a busy guy, lots of people to judge, all that. Also, I needed a nap."

"So there's sleep in the afterlife?"

"Not for the wicked."

Fred was starting to worry. He'd always believed that he was living a good life, but when you factor in the details, it looked a little less rosy.

"OK, first off, Fred, I've got a tally of how many women you slept with and I'm sorry to say that you just didn't bag enough chicks to get in. The magic number is twenty, Fred. Sorry."

Now Fred was sweating, metaphorically of course. There's no perspiration in heaven. That's why angels don't need deodorant.

"Kidding, Fred. God doesn't keep a sex log. He's not a pimp. But, you're nervous . . . and with good reason. Let's look at some of the good things you did, Fred . . . well, there's not that much. And damn, dude, your life was pretty boring. You never even went to Europe."

"I went to Las Vegas."

"Yeah, like *that's* going to get you into heaven. OK, I'm scanning, scanning. Fred, what was the deal with your neighbor's dog when you were seven? I'm seeing that you used to taunt him until he basically committed suicide."

"Dogs can kill themselves?"

"Yeah. Suicide is losing the will to live, bro. That's it. You little people haven't realized yet that the brain controls the body. You go see all those freaking doctors and you take their stupid little pills, and they only work, most of them, because you <u>think</u> they're going to work. But, generally speaking, you're just as well off eating hamster pellets. It's in the brain, not the stethoscope."

"But they've got those lab coats."

"That they do, Fred. That they do. Let's check out your early life, OK. You did make Becky Yarbrough cry when you were six, but making six-year-old girls cry isn't all that bad. Hey, she showed you hers, but you didn't show her yours. Fred, that's not very nice."

"Send me back for a minute. I'll show her mine."

"No, Fred, that's called exposing yourself, and it's much less cute when you're in your fifties. You were a pretty good teenager, compared to most, but you ratted out your friend, Brian, when you two got caught with that bottle of tequila in tenth grade."

"I told the truth."

"You did, but you people never got the whole bear false witness commandment. I mean, come on, it doesn't say no lies, it says no false witness. It's a freaking legal term, Fred. We just didn't want people getting put in jail. We weren't stupid enough to think that you guys weren't going to lie. Come on, we are, you know, <u>higher</u> <u>powers</u>."

"So, I should have lied?"

"You're missing the point, Fred. You shouldn't have ratted out your friend. You also probably shouldn't have masturbated so many times to your aunt Helen. For now, let's talk about how many times you got busted touching yourself. Fred, this is a truly amazing number . . . and, by such a wide variety of people. Most teenage boys get busted by their mothers at some point, but you got busted by an employee at Burger King. At Burger King, come on, Fred, have some pride."

"But isn't that a deadly sin?"

"Sure, but, dude, Burger King? That's just gross, Fred. You also got busted by two junior high school teachers, a janitor, a rent-a-cop and the mayor. Fred you touched yourself in City Hall? My Lord. Moving on, your career was a bust, Fred, my man."

"What do you mean?"

"I mean God hates accountants, just hates them. Basically He hates anybody who makes money for the sake of making money."

"So money's bad?"

"No, money's not bad. It's not good. It's just money, stuff. And, despite spending a lifetime zealously pursuing it, you made surprisingly little of it.

You don't remember the whole eye of the needle, camel thing? It's debtor's hell for you."

"Oh my God."

"Fred, lighten up. I'm a joker. I'm a midnight toker."

"You get high?"

"There's great weed up here, dude . . . hydroponic, obviously."

"But my preacher said it was sinful . . . I just wanted to live right."

"You barely lived, Fred."

"But I never tried gay stuff. I went to church every week, sometimes twice a week. I voted however my preacher told me to vote. I didn't take too many names in vain."

"Did you even read the Bible, Fred? Where does it say anything about dressing up and sitting in a building with your neighbors pretending to be pious? What makes you think that God cares about who you sleep with?"

"Um, my preacher, Deuteronomy, um . . ."

"Don't even get me started."

"Sorry. What religion was I supposed to be?"

"Zoroastrian . . . no, man, it doesn't matter. God doesn't particularly like Southern Baptists, but even some of them are in here. The gossip is that the ones that are in hell have to attend gay marriage ceremonies over and over for all eternity . . . heh, heh, you've got to give Satan credit for creativity. He's also a hell of a cook."

"So, what can I do to make up for all that I did wrong?"

"Well Fred, you can try again, my brother. I don't know why the early Christians cut out the whole reincarnation thing. I think it's cool, but, either way, you're going back."

"As a cockroach?"

"Nope."

"As a chicken?"

"No dude, but that was funny. You're going back as a person. You've been given a second chance, technically a twenty-fifth chance, but I like you, Fred. I really do. So, this time, enjoy His gifts, be a good man, try and live it to the fullest, and for God's sake, man, don't touch yourself at Burger King."

THE ONGOING ADVENTURES OF . . . , part ten

THE ONGOING ADVENTURES OF SOUTHERN FOOD

Southern food enjoyed a brief stint of popularity. It was delicious and, apparently, good for the soul. However, eventually people began to realize that deep frying lettuce isn't the healthiest culinary option around.

THE ONGOING ADVENTURES OF SOUTHERN GUILT

Sorry, mom.

THE ONGOING ADVENTURES OF THE CANADIAN GANGSTA

Bradley Thompson was a bad ass, or he would've been if curse words had been allowed in Canada. He was, instead, a bad butt. He could make gang signs in French as well as English. He knew fifty ways to kill a moose. And, yeah, he did wear a solid color, but it was orange, and that was because he was also a crossing guard, the baddest butt crossing guard on the West siiiddee of Alberta. Believe dat.

THE ONGOING ADVENTURES OF BAD SPIN-OFFS

Felix Gold had grown up fascinated by the lives of musicians. From an early age, Felix had planned to, when he grew up, launch a TV show where we can see the lives of musicians, what lies just behind the music. Unfortunately, VH-1 stole his idea. But not being one to give up on his dreams, and not being one to be particularly creative, Felix came up with the idea for Behind the Muzac. He interviewed the production engineers who removed the words from Billy Ocean and Madonna songs. It . . . wasn't all that good.

THE ONGOING ADVENTURES OF THE ONVERZEALOUS LOTTERY WINNER

"Oh my God! This is the best moment of my life. I've got to call my cousin, Rose, and tell her that I just won fifteen dollars!! This is amazing. I sometimes like to punch midgets in the face for no reason. Oh, dear God. Thank you, thank you! This is better than the time at Sea World when I molested that dolphin! I've prayed for this moment all my life. I can't believe that I won! I won! Me, the girl who once shot a panda. I won. I beat all of you! Those fifteen dollars are all mine. I'm going to buy new brake pads for my son's wheelie shoes. My God! I won! I won! This is the pinnacle of my sad, sad existence. I won! I beat out all of you! I'd like to apologize to my priest for fondling him. I won! I just can't contain my excitement! Yes! Yes!"

NOBODY KNOWS BUT MICKEY

Bill R. Keyes had been to jail. In fact, he's been on the inside of so many American justice centers, that he's written a travelogue. It's informative, if you want to know how many Mormon members of Sur Trece there are in San Quinton or the best way to protect your corn hole in the Mississippi State pen. Yeah, a person would be hard-pressed not to call Bill an expert in this particular sub-field of sociological self-preservation. But, the Disney jail was a unique experience, even for a man as familiar with incarceration as Bill.

Having long since had his passport revoked, Bill was curious about other countries, their cultures, their rituals and what stereotypical, dancing, animatronic representations of that culture might look like. So, naturally, he went to Epcot Center. If you want to learn about other countries, but not really, there's no place like Epcot.

But while watching some fake Japanese robots perform hari-kari on themselves for sneezing in the middle of a business presentation and thus shaming their families for generations to come, Bill got a little angry. And this wasn't your normal Disney "I can't believe I'm paying fifty dollars for this crap" anger. This was ex-con anger—this was a guy who'd once fought off a gang of horny Haitians with a used spork anger—this was the world's scariest reality show anger. Bill felt slighted. In the midst of a fit of largely misdirected rage, Bill began ripping the heads off of Japanese themed robots and angrily hurling them toward Australia.

It wasn't long before Disney's crack security squad came and subdued Bill with waffle-cone-shaped tear gas canisters and candy-cane striped Billy clubs. Disney is all about not making children cry, unless they happen to chance upon the Gay Day parade. And the Disney Super-Duper Fun Facility, also known as a holding cell, is unique. First off, in accordance with its bylaws, all of the jailers are dressed as Disney characters. The bosses didn't want to chance having a stray kid see actual security personnel. So, brilliantly, they decided that the jailers should be dressed like almost every other employee. Bill was dragged to the Super-Duper Fun Facility by Goofy and Clara Belle, the female cow character who makes absolutely no sense, except perhaps to give Goofy someone to fuck. Bill R. Keyes was beaten repeatedly by Goofy, which is not only the most surreal thing that would happen to Bill in his life, but also really funny . . . even to him . . . even while it was happening. Sure the Billy Clubs hurt, but getting your ass kicked by Goofy, that's funny.

The jailers are also required to be perky and friendly, even while discharging their duties. Thus, when a happy Midwestern nuclear family of four saw Clara Belle beating Bill with steel candy canes, the two kids wanted in on that action, and ran towards them, curious. Of course, Goofy was required to dance for the kids while Clara Belle continued the beating. Then Goofy joined in on the beating, being aware enough to add "boing" noises to cover Bill's screams of pain. Luckily, the kids soon lost interest when they saw a really big bee fly by. And Goofy stopped his rage fueled beat-down when Clara Belle reminded him, "Gawrsh, Goofy, you're going to damage his internal organs."

Once in the Super-Duper Fun Facility, Bill and the other inmate were treated to a lunch of five pounds of leftover cotton candy (a form of torture in and of itself). Bill's cellie was there for exposing himself to puppets, a definite no-no in Disney World and DisneyLand, though strangely encouraged in Euro Disney.

Chapter Seventeen of Bill's *Prison Pal* book states—"Disney Jail is weird. You know it's going to be weird, but the CO's have to wear those big cartoon suits even when they're inside and out of view of the kids. I think it's because Disney has more cameras than most casinos." Bill goes on to say that the real cops who inevitably come and pick you up from the Disney cops can't even keep a straight face when the Disney guys read off the perp's offenses. Who could?

BABY NAMES

The Jones' were sick of being put on the spot. Every time that Mrs. Jennie May Jones had a new baby (roughly every ten months), she and her husband had to think of a baby name right there on the spot. Their fifth child wound up being named Speculum.

It was December. Jim Jameson Jones had just returned from "the plant" where he works. His wife, Mrs. Jennie May Jones, was in her third trimester. And they'd long since run through the easy names. They even solicited help, going so far as to call their rich, lottery winning, distant cousins over in Comment, GA, who had no good advice for the expectant couple. So, tonight Jim and Jennie May were going to sit down at the kitchen table and come up with a list of names for their next twelve kids, provided Mrs. Jones' uterus doesn't explode before then.

"Aiight Jennie, tonight's the night. Let's get at er."

"Well, what about Freda? That was my aunt's name you know."

"Naw, too Yankee sounding."

"OK, Scarlett?"

"Well, it's not Yankee, but we've already got three girls named Scarlett."

"Oh yeah. Hey, I've got it. Go and fetch our Bible. They've got all kinds of names in there."

"Here it is. Where's the baby names section?"

"Just turn to any page."

"OK, I've got Haggai, and Zerub'babel."

"No."

"OK. I've got She-al'ti-el."

"What's that mean?"

"Nothin'. It's a name, and one we ain't used yet."

"Too weird. Try another page."

"OK, I've got Damascus and Ahaz."

"Ahaz? You want me to name my baby Ahaz? Forget the Bible. What other books we got?"

"A cookbook."

"Good idea honey, let's call him Broccoli."

"Well no, but maybe Couscous."

"I kinda like that one, but the kids'll make fun of him."

"OK, Casserole?"

"No."

"Rigatoni?"

"No."

"Angel Hair?"

"Yeah. That's one. Good, keep going."

"All right. Frappe'?"

"Not bad."

"Uh, Gelatin?"

"No."

"Brunswick Stew?"

"Stew? You want Stew?"

"Could be short fer Stewart."

"Yeah, but it's not. It's short for Brunswick Stew. OK, enough with the cookbook. What other books we got?"

"Does hunting magazines count? Epidural left one in the bathroom."

"Couldn't hurt."

"OK, honey, what about Four Pointer?"

"No."

"Buck?"

"Buck. I can deal with Buck."

"Good, cause my next one was Desert Camouflage, but we'll just try somethin' else. I've got a Sports Illustrated. What about naming him after that golfer, the really good one, the black guy?"

"Tiger Woods?"

"Yeah. Tiger Woods Jones. Maybe. Who else's in there?"

"Rasheed? Dante? World B. Free?"

"Dante's good. Grab that fishing magazine that Forceps left on the counter."

"OK, we've got Small Mouth, Blue Gill, Carp?"

"I kind of like Blue Gill."

"Yeah, but you really want to name the kid after a color? That's like naming him Orange."

And the spirited debate lasted all night, right up until the time that Jennie's water broke and they had to send their oldest son, C-Section, for the doctor. They wound up calling the next kid Junior. It's just easier that way.

PULL AROUND TO THE SECOND WINDOW

From the first time that she ordered a Whopper Junior at the local Burger King and was told to pull around, Kelly Bradley knew that the drive-thru was going to be a part of her destiny. She didn't know quite how or quite why, but, for some reason, the idea of a drive-thru just captured her imagination. Since that day, Kelly was determined to run a business with a drive-thru, preferably one with two windows.

But there were already too many drive-thru restaurants. There are drive-thru pharmacies, drive-thru banks, even drive-thru liquor stores in Texas (which is a monumentally bad idea, but then again, so is Texas). Kelly wanted to create a business with a drive-thru, but she didn't really care what type of business it was. Since she'd inherited a whole bunch of settlement money when her parents died in that disastrous incident when the K fell off of the K-Mart, flattening four people and a deaf seeing-eye dog, Kelly had the resources. Now she just needed an idea.

Kelly loved shoes. So, naturally, a drive-thru shoe store was her first foray into the exciting world of drive-thru retail. But, she didn't think that one all the way through. The customers would drive up and scan the shoe menu, telling the employee on the other end of the microphone which pair they wanted and in what size. Then they'd drive up to the first window and receive the shoes. The customers were then supposed to try on the shoes between the first and second windows, and, if they wanted them, pay for them at the second window. Unfortunately, Kelly didn't realize that a lot of people would just get the shoes and drive off. That was a problem, but not nearly as much of a problem as the fact that it's damn near impossible try on shoes and drive. After the second three-car pile-up, Kelly's Quick Shoes was dead.

But that didn't dampen Kelly's passion for the drive-thru phenomenon. She just decided to change products. Keeping the same building, Kelly spun the wheel of capitalism. Her drive-thru Taxidermy Store was an interesting experiment—"Quality Stuffed Dead Animals in About an Hour" led to a lot of angry rednecks and a lawsuit from some optometry outfit with a similar slogan. Kelly's Drive-Thru Tattoo and Piercing Parlor was just bizarre. It didn't last long. You'd be surprised how tough it is to keep your foot on the brake when someone's piercing your nipple.

The two months that Kelly's Drive-Thru Sperm Bank was open were the most random, and possibly most exciting, of Kelly's life. At the first window the donor was given a cup, some paper towels, and the pornography of his or her choice. He or she was then told to pull over to one of the designated Masturbation Spaces to fill the cup by any means necessary. At the second window they gave their seed to the teller and got money in return. If the cops had let Kelly put up her big drive-in porno movie screen in the Masturbation Lot, the clinic might've lasted longer. And being located next to a day care center, it wasn't long before a disgusted mother complained that there was a line of cars facing the day care facility, all of them with men furiously masturbating inside. Another noble drive-thru experiment failed, but still Kelly was undeterred. She knew that it was just a matter of time before she chanced upon the right product.

Since she was already next to a day care center, the next idea was a drive-thru discipline service. Kelly really thought that this one might work. And it should have. You see, white people don't spank their kids anymore, which is a shame since most of them desperately need to be spanked. So, Kelly offered her services. The mother would drive up to the menu spot and tell the invisible employee what the child did wrong, and what she wanted the kid to be spanked with. The choices were: palm, doubled over leather belt, two-by-four, two-by-four with fake rusty nail on end (for the scare factor), magazine, switch, Billy club, dead cat, wiffle bat, and wooden paddle. Except for the discomfort of the mother who had to hold her kid in her lap with his or her butt facing out the window, it was a good idea. People liked it, but Kelly hardly got any repeat business, since after the kid got spanked with a dead cat once, the threat was then usually enough to shut the kid up in the future. So, Kelly's House of Discipline folded too, but the website still gets hundreds of disappointed hits a day.

Kelly's final idea was a drive-thru advice parlor. She was almost broke, but still had enough resources to hire a priest, a psychologist, a general practitioner, a CPA, a rabbi, Ken Jennings of Jeopardy fame, a swami, a stern grandmother with a good memory, a guru, and a leading Richard

Simmons clone. People would drive up and choose from the advisor menu, then drive up to the first window where they'd ask their question. By the time they got to the second window, the advisor would have some handy, pithy nugget of advice, most of which they got from a Speak and Spell or a bathroom wall. Still, Kelly's Drive-Thru Advice and All was enough of a success not to get sued or shut down by the police. So, if you're in existential trouble, if no one else can help, and if you can find the time, then maybe you can hire the A-team, or if not, then try Kelly's.

THE DOCTOR RIORDAN PLAN

"Hello. I'm Doctor Jonathan Riordan, psychologist. Is your child defiant? Does he or she listen to you? Does your child have problems with behavior, ADHD, or acting out in school? Well, I'm here to tell you there's a solution. With my plan of a vitamin based diet, daily hugs, and intense shock therapy, I can turn your defiant kid into one who listens to you and does whatever you say. It's really an ancient parenting technique known colloquially as 'scaring the shit out of your child' or STSOYC . . . and it works."

Doctor Jonathan Riordan was an entrepreneur at heart. Despite earning a medical degree in order to placate his mother, Jonathan was a salesman in his soul. Some people are just born to sell, and he was one. Being a psychologist in the early 21st century means that, like all other businesses, you basically have to advertise. Luckily, Dr. Riordan knew how to captivate an audience. He never got that whole "do no harm" thing, but since when has that ever limited anyone's success in America?

"Hello. I'm Doctor Jonathan Riordan, psychologist. Do you have trouble losing weight? Have you dieted and dieted and dieted and never achieved the desired results? Are you afraid to go swimming or look at yourself in the mirror naked? Well, I'm here to tell you that there's an answer. Until the advent of modern medicine, many women chose to lose weight the natural way, through tapeworms. I say, why not bring tapeworms into the 21st century? For only four payments of $39.99, I will send you five adult tapeworms, a worm farm to house them, some pudding to eat them with, and an instructional video entitled, "I Just Ate Some Tapeworms, Now What?" See the results you've wanted all of your life. Don't settle for being overweight. Lose weight the natural way, without expensive drugs, calorie counting, or starvation. Join the tapeworm revolution. Lose weight and gain a friend for life. Call today."

Dr. Jonathan Riordan didn't specialize in one area of psychology or another. He wanted to do it all, and find a way to charge for it. In a sense, he was a modern doctor (no conscience required). In another sense, he was more of a throw-back (he made house calls and was a sort of one-man traveling medicine show). Dr. Riordan was an opportunist.

"Do you ever feel rushed? Is there ever enough time in the day to do all that you need to do? Do you ever wish that you could just slow down? Well, now you can. Hello, I'm Doctor Jonathan Riordan, psychologist, and I've recently discovered the secret to slowing down. My new pill, Relaxarimeron, is a mixture of the ground pineal gland of a three-toed South American tree sloth, acetaminophen, Omega-3 fatty acids, and opium. Believe me, it **will** slow you down. But don't take my word for it, listen to this: 'My name is Jenny Skidlow. I used to be rushed all the time. I'm an air traffic controller, which is a high-stress job, and, even when I wasn't working, I used to feel constant nervousness and worry, but after I started Dr. Riordan's program of sloth brains and intense narcotic use, I don't worry about much of anything anymore. In fact, I don't think I'm wearing pants.' See folks, it's just that easy."

Dr. Riordan got into a little trouble for that one.

I GET A CALL FROM MY BROTHER
(a true story . . . for the most part)

So, I was just waking up on what I had thought was going to be a relaxing, lazy Saturday. I'd already brushed my teeth, taken a little fake half-bath in the sink, and was putting on deodorant when he called.

"Tim, quick, get your ass over here. My car's on fire."

You know, there are few utterances which can motivate you to jump in your car in your boxers and wife-beater and speed away faster than mentioning the word "fire". It's like when you get the calls mentioning "fellatio Thursday," or "the stick is blue".

Switching tenses, I do manage to put on shoes and grab my keys. As I'm rushing out of my crappy apartment complex, I steal the fire extinguisher from off the wall. Driving the 12 short blocks from my apartment to my brother and his wife's house, I couldn't help but think of the last time one of us was on fire. That time it was me instead of my brother's car, and I was in a 7-11 parking lot, so this time wasn't quite as intense, and there were fewer Slurpees involved, but it was weirder.

A LITTLE BACKGROUND

My brother, Pete, and his wife, Elaine, are newlyweds. They're of the emotional, dramatic school. They fight and make up, and then fight and make up, and then . . .

Some couples are boring. This one isn't. They live in a quaint, little duplex at the top of a hill in a cozy, suburban middle-class neighborhood. The driveway is like a ski jump, it's so steep. You actually have to use your emergency brake when you park, a fact that I, understandably, forgot when I saw my brother at the top of the driveway trying in vain to smack a raging car fire out with a highly-flammable broom. I parked the car, grabbed the extinguisher, and jumped out.

I saw Pete in a singed pin-striped suit repeatedly hitting some flaming jumper cables with a broom. This only fanned the flame. Pete's wife, Elaine, was in a nightgown, standing off to one side, yelling at him, and God, and the jumper cables.

My brother yelled, "Tim, get over here."

My sister-in-law yelled, "Tim, your car."

Then all three of us, even the one currently on fire, paused to watch my brown Toyota Camry roll down the steep driveway, through the street, and into the woods on the other side. Then we went back to the matter at hand.

"Dude, you're on fire."

Pete noticed.

"Stop, drop and roll."

"But it's my good suit."

Elaine and I grabbed him, threw him down and patted out the fire. Then Pete leapt up, snagged the fire extinguisher from off the ground and aimed it at the cables. The fire was now spreading toward the car (you know those things that run on gasoline), making this a pretty urgent matter.

"What the f."

"Pull the pin."

"What?"

"Like a grenade."

We'd both been really into GI Joe, so we figured that we had enough military know-how to properly operate a grenade. Pete got the pin out and then aimed the smelly shaving cream stream toward the cables. The fire went out. We were safe . . . for now . . . except for my car.

THE MIRACLE ON RON'S ASS

That crazy Virgin Mary . . . She pops up everywhere. We've seen her lounging on half-cooked tortillas, hanging out inside of avocados, mysteriously appearing as a part of a large lichen mold while playing Rock-Paper-Scissors with Elvis. But, this is the first time in recorded history that the Virgin Mary had appeared on a gay man's ass.

It wasn't as if Ron Shoemaker had asked for a birthmark to appear out of nowhere on his thirtieth birthday. And, even if it had been a wish of his to have a pseudo-religious beauty mark, he wouldn't have wanted it on his ass. I mean, his ass was one of the things Ron took pride in, as evidenced by the Herculean numbers of lunges he did daily and the fact that Ron Shoemaker was one of the handful of people in recorded medical history to have received a butt lift at age 27.

Still, despite his desires and the fact that it defied all medical logic, there She was, just hanging out on Ron's left cheek. The Madonna seemed unfazed, understandably, since she'd appeared in stranger places.

But, they say that life is different in the 21st century, and it is, in a way. In the past, when the Mother of God had appeared in a strange place, the Church would cover it up, or dismiss the founder as a quack. This is not as easy to do nowadays since, A—a lot more folks are skeptical of the Pope and his wacky clan these days as a rule, and B—everybody's got a camera. So even if the Catholics wanted to cover up Ron's ass mark, Ron's friends had no problems taking pictures of his butt and then broadcasting it to the world. And once your ass gets out onto the Internet, it's there to stay.

In the past it had been a relatively simple matter for the Church to hush up something it didn't want out there. When Jesus showed up for his long-awaited second coming, but did so as a hard-drinking Buddhist garbage man, it went away fast. When The Virgin had appeared in that pile of elephant dung at the North Carolina Zoo, well, the Church didn't exactly advertise it on the Vatican News Network (you know, VNN). And when an image of Satan appeared on the Pope's pancreas, let's just say that that X-ray mysteriously disappeared.

But Ron's butt was now a story, and not merely a tabloid one. The major international news outlets descended on Helen's Hollow, Georgia, like a plague of locusts (actually a decent press analogy if you think about it). Mayor Horace W. Pendershoe and Deputy Mayor Bo had to act like they were excited about the press coverage and corresponding tourist dollars that might soon be heading their way, but really Helen's Hollow is a small town that's happy to stay that way.

For the residents of this happy, small town, the Virgin could not have appeared on a worse butt cheek. Every small town has got at least one gay couple, even if the couple and the town won't admit it. It's one of those "chuckle and move on" rural American phenomena. But when your small town is now known as both a Christian Mecca and a homosexual one, then it's like vacationing in Las Vegas, Sudan—it might be weird, it'll definitely be funny, and somebody's going to die.

One thing which constantly amazes me about America is how fast we can jump on a trend and then how fast we can run that sucker into the ground. The Ron's *Ahem* Museum of Spirituality was up before you could say "why?" The City Council did debate the name of the museum for over an hour so as not to offend any tourist dollars, I mean, tourists, no matter what their religious and/or sexual orientation.

And the tourists did come, in their expected droves. Fresh-faced families of four who looked like they stepped out of a post card for Middle America flocked to Helen's Hollow like there was gold in them there butt cheeks. This was great for Randy's Pharmacy, Penelope's Eatery and the city's bottom line (no pun intended), and only really bad for the Catholic Church and Ron's lower back.

Ron's emerging scoliosis was an issue, but another, broader issue, was that Helen's Hollow had never been a tourist town before. And it wasn't given a grace period to ease into it. Being a small tourist town is different than being a non-tourist small town. You have to look clean, safe, and interesting. If your town has a town drunk (Helen's Hollow's is named Sammy Kilfinger), you might need to start hiding him, unless he's a funny drunk. Sammy Kilfinger is not a funny drunk. He is, however, a rapey drunk, and that's why he's going to stay in jail until the Ron's ass phenomenon blows over.

Father Diego Ramirez had never been to the rural South, and, after his current posting, he would make it his mission never to go back, although he did take a piece of the South with him, eventually quitting the priesthood to open Spain's first deep-fried Twinkie stand. If you've ever seen a movie, you know what the Vatican does when it encounters things like Ron's Miracle Anus. It sends out a skeptical emissary to either prove the event wrong, a hoax, a mistake, or, occasionally, a miracle.

When Father Diego was sent to Portugal to determine if a 10-year-old boy had stigmata, he eventually came to the conclusion that the kid was just a creative hemophiliac. When El Padre was sent to Chile to determine if Jesus' face had appeared on the inside of a thrice-baked potato, he was hard pressed to definitively say "no, this is definitely a fraud." And Father Ramirez had to acquiesce on the 6-year-old Mexican girl who spoke perfect Pig-Aramaic. But there was simply no way that Father Diego Ramirez was going to allow a miracle to happen on a sodomite's ass cheek . . . . and so, he didn't. It took some hypnotherapy, a Brillo pad and some industrial-strength solvent, but at least Holy Mother Church didn't have open that can of sexually-repressed worms.

So the Church narrowly avoided yet another major controversy. Helen's Hollow, Georgia, did garner some additional revenue (although building the giant statue of Ron's Holy Rectum is now generally thought of as a mistake). And Ron and his friends remember this as a funny, and random, memory. Unfortunately, the post-scrubbed birthmark looks kind of like Mohammed and Mary Magdalene playing with a dreidel.

A HOUSE DIVIDED

Theodore and Nancy Vignaccio had a great marriage . . . for about ten years. In today's world that's a pretty long time for a marriage to function as well, as seamlessly, as square peggish in square holeish, as theirs had. But, as the poets, porn stars and volcano-virgins say, "all good things must come to an end".

The Vignaccios' marital troubles wouldn't have been that big of a deal if they hadn't been successful business partners. You see, if a couple starts a business which takes off and then they split up personally, they could either try and keep the business going together but live separate personal lives, one of them could sell, or both of them could sell. But, there was only one option for the Vignaccios. You see, they were both inventors by trade. That's how they met. It was at an invention convention. Locking eyes across a room crowded with battery-powered baby strollers, computers made from Canadian tree bark, and spec cars that run on scalloped potatoes, Theodore and Nancy immediately connected. It was mystical. It was exciting. It was love.

Together, the newly married Vignaccios decided to pool their creative resources, take out a loan, and start a business. If you've ever had insomnia, done too many drugs, or somehow else found yourself staring at a late night infomercial, then you've probably seen an equally stocky, swarthy man-and-wife team with heavy Brooklyn accents hawking their inventive wares. That's the Vignaccios. He even has a catch-phrase, but it's not catchy enough to remember.

For ten years the Vignaccios brainstormed, planned, and pieced together their dreams. They invented the first juicer designed specifically for meat products. Although a strange invention, it did gain relative popularity in West Virginia and even spawned a short-lived trend of other liquid meat product spin-offs, such as Chickenade and 'Gin and Pork Juice'. If you've never had a veal shank frappe', then you haven't lived.

Building on their modicum of fame, the Vignaccios soon released the first All-American King's English-to-Redneck Electronic Dictionary. It was supposed to be a way to bring North and South together and expand Nascar's popularity base. And some naïve New England/Florida beach bunnies even bought a few, although more than a few bait shop owners in the Carolinas did wonder why someone from Connecticut needed a translator. Then they shrugged and jacked up the price of crickets.

Moving past their sophomore slump, the Vignaccios went on to invent a few things you've actually heard of, and maybe even used, over the next decade. They were the power couple who came up with the idea for the telekinetically-responsive wheelchair (not allowed at The Special Olympics, post-scandal). Building on the popularity of the edible bread bowl for soups and chili, the Vignaccios came out with an entire line of edible utensils. The Vegemite Glassware wasn't a hit, but the Spoonausage did sell. Their sporks made out of frozen, high-fructose corn syrup did earn them a great deal of money, but America's always had a weird, incestuous relationship with corn.

The Vignaccios were also the team which came up with the Pogo Elevator, the Street Wine Koozie, and the Greek Theater Ski Masks (for the classically-trained convenience store burglar). Yes, it cannot be denied that the Vignaccios did produce a few items which made their way into our collective consciousness. Theodore and Nancy played off of each other so brilliantly on television that, seeing them, you had the feeling that they were in love . . . and they were . . . until Nancy caught Theodore with five Laotian prostitutes, an industrial-sized bucket of Vaseline, and one confused toy poodle who seemed relieved to be rescued. This event effectively ended the Vignaccios' marriage. But neither Nancy nor Theodore was short-sighted enough to let bubbling anger, marital resentment, or diseased regret ruin a successful business.

So the business went on. The infomercials continued. And the inventions kept coming. But something was different now.

The first post-divorce late-night infomercial pretty well explained the strange new direction the Vignaccios' business had taken. When Theodore introduced the world to Earth's first curling iron in history that tells women that they're fat and that no one will ever love them, the audience was intrigued. When Nancy proudly displayed the world's largest condom and marketed it to women as an intimate way to say to your soon-to-be ex-husband that your new body-building, college-aged lover left these here last night, the audience nervously laughed. By the time Theodore fired back with his newly copy written female-baldness-inducing hairspray, the live studio audience was pretty well freaked out. Usually you can count on those live studio audience losers to gasp, sigh, and shriek with delight on cue (granted, that probably has something to do with the off—camera neon sign that tells them what to do and the fact that they're losers). But tonight's audience was not responding to the usual stimuli. They were beginning to squirm and a few of them made their way to the exits.

By the time Theodore had shown us his Rufinol Bonbons and Nancy had shown us the first beer specifically brewed to cause genital shrinkage, the audience had, somewhat ironically, migrated over to the studio where they film The Family Feud. Ahh, The Family Feud, it's like death and taxes. It's something you can count on. You can also count on it sucking, but, unlike the Vignaccios, at least it's consistent.

MASCULINITY

The small town of Heart, Mississippi, was hurting for tourism. Despite the fact that the world's second largest ball of snot is located in Heart, tourists have mysteriously stopped visiting and leaving their tourist dollars. On the day that that small Indonesian village announced that its snot ball is, in fact, larger in diameter and sheer volume of nasal drippage, you could hear the town of Heart begin its long, slow death rattle.

A few years after they were knocked off the Guinness mantle, the townsfolk elected their favorite shop keep and tall tale teller, Peter Peterson, mayor. Peter ran on a pro-snot platform, whereas his opponent, a shrewish CPA named Mary Manning, ran a distinctly anti-mucus campaign. Mary wanted to offer tax breaks to companies to entice them to come to Heart, set up shop, and provide jobs. She also wanted to lower property taxes and work to limit greenhouse gas emissions in the city limit. The people wanted none of that.

Peter's plan, known locally as Peter's Plan, was simple. Heart would regain its former glory through committed teamwork in the town, which he called townwork. Each day, the residents of Heart were to pass by City Hall and leave their family's collected snot in the drop box. The people were to harvest their own snot, by any means necessary, and then drop it off in front of City Hall, so that the Commissioner of Nasal Refuse could organize the local Snotballers Union 417 and begin work on a second snotball.

The plan failed.

After Peter's plan had been officially decried as a huge failure, and while the residents of Heart were wondering what they should now do with their excess snot, other ideas surfaced. Heartians, it seemed, had their collective creative juices flowing from having banded together as a community for the first time since the Great Choctaw Banishing of Ought Four (an event wisely left out of the history books).

Jenny McFarthing, the local school produce purveyor, had the idea of building an amusement park to compete with the Six Flags in Texas. Thomas Ingle thought that Heart should try and create a giant heart-shaped bed of roses that could be seen from space like the Great Wall of China. But he was gay, so nobody in Mississippi cared.

The Reverend Joseph McNickle said that we needed to make Heart an Evangelical Mecca for Christians who felt that the secular world was just too darn full of sinnin' and body glitter. He suggested that the town leaders design a new town based entirely on conservative Christian principles, ban all liquor sales and replace them with massive amounts of grape juice, ban Thomas Ingle and his "tennis buddy" (effectively destroying the Heart gay community), chain all women of marrying age to whichever kitchen appliance is closest, and replace all laws with the Ten Commandments. His idea was popular but then they remembered that Branson, Missouri, already did that and that Branson's more than a little creepy.

Finally the Heart police force threw their two cents in. America has become too feminized. Let's make Heart a masculine city, a city where a man is free to be a man and not a cloistered eunuch who jumps when his wife says jump and shops at Bed, Bath and Beyond.

Sergeant Kip Linderson pointed out that America doesn't have a Pamplonaesque event where men can test their masculinity and possibly be gored by an enraged animal. They could have their own Running of the Bulls. There are some bulls in Mississippi and they could even import new bulls. But then Chief Tice said that they should do something original and the other cops, fearing to disagree with the chief, agreed. Officer Patrick noted that there are also a lot of chickens in Mississippi. They could have a Running of the Chickens. But that didn't seem very manly. They could have a Running of the Cocks, which, while popular with Thomas Ingle and his "tennis buddy", still failed to garner sufficient support. The rookie suggested tumbleweeds. Oklahoma was looking to unload some of its excess tumbleweeds, so Mississippi offered to trade Brett Favre's hometown for a "whole mess of tumbleweeds". The ASPCA doesn't list tumbleweeds as endangered yet, so they're really cheap, even in barter terms. Although it might not have been the most masculine idea, it was the beginning of a tradition. And now, if you're bored in Heart, Mississippi, and if you can't find a liquor store, then you too can participate in the Annual Running of the Tumbleweeds.

POOPNOSTICATION

The year was 1968. Social revolution was in the air. Musicians and activists were challenging people to look at the world differently. The world was changing. And I was on the shitter.

I didn't immediately come to the conclusion that now seems so simple, so obvious. Like most of us modern thinkers, I'd considered augury and auspices (divination from birds and animal livers) as a quaint, but stupid, practice of the past. It was pre-science and, therefore, wrong. But it turns out that I was the quaint, stupid one.

The first time that I realized that I had the power to predict the future from careful examination of my own turds, I was pretty drunk. Otherwise, I probably never would've sat staring at the full toilet bowl for two hours, and I never would've thought that my log was telling me to invest in organic produce. But, as I was later to realize, sometimes the shading of the turd is as important as the shape and substance.

Sure, that first one was easy. Anyone can look at their crap and say, "Hey, it's too green. I need to cut down on the dairy." But it takes special insight to realize, "Hey, that third ridge is slightly tilted toward the magnetic North Pole. We need to bomb Cambodia." In retrospect, I never should've called Henry Kissinger.

My cousin, Sharon, the hippie, was in Chicago during that fateful Democratic Convention. I tried to get in touch with her to tell her not to attend the demonstration, but, in those innocent, pre-cell phone, days, it just wasn't possible to let her know that I'd seen 14 peanuts spelling out the words, "Cuz in trouble" in that morning's dump. If only I could've contacted her, she might not be the lesbian prison bitch she is today.

My mother lost her cornea in a freak bridge accident (the seven of spades flew out of Liza Joe Simpson, her partner's, hand and cut her eye on a particularly ruff trick). I'd warned her not to play that day after seeing

7 partially digested corn nuggets in the shape of a spade in my morning bowl. But mothers never listen.

I also correctly predicted the 1969 Southern California flood from an especially painful case of diarrhea. I later saw the 1980 Mount Saint Helens volcanic eruption in its precursor form (my toilet exploded, raining some pretty nasty stuff onto the linoleum, killing exactly 57 G.I. Joe figures my son had left in the bathroom). As I was spanking him with a Wiffle Bat, I figured that I'd better call FEMA. But once again, no one believed the Poopnosticator.

Will "science" ever recognize the importance of my feces? Will the mainstream ever realize that God has chosen my rectum as the backdrop for divine messages? Will my wife ever rescind the restraining order? Time will tell.

. . . AND WE'RE NOT GOING TO TAKE IT ANYMORE

The people were fed up. They had noticed the ever-so-subtle changes in the country and it made them squirmy. They saw their golden Utopia slipping further and further away from them. They saw the future. They didn't like what it looked like . . . and they weren't going to take it anymore.

First it was subtle—Velcro replacing the shoelace on the occasional tennis shoe brand. OK, whatever. The kids like it and it's novel. Then they saw Velcro slowly begin to replace plastic buttons on baseball caps, which elicited a growing sense of wary suspicion. That was when fashion designer Werner Johansen Garcia came out with his "fall line". Velcro had replaced the buttons on this year's line of marginally-different-from-last-year's-rehashed-they-really-think-women-are-this-stupid blouses. And it caught on. The PTA lamented it. Strippers loved it. And teenaged American girls proved yet again that they have no sales resistance. Sure, a few discerning fashion writers saw it as the trick it was, but the idea was already firmly planted in the minds of Middle America. The cliché slogan wrote itself— "Velcro is the new button."

Soon the cable news shouters noticed. Insane asylum inmate-of-the-month-turned-political-"news"-anchor, Greg O'Dooley, took up the button cause with a vengeance.

"Wake up, people. It's everywhere. At first it was just a Velcro hat here or a tennis shoe there, but now it's in the schools. Your kids are going to school with Velcro. I just read that the Kansas City school district reports that young girls have created a system that tells boys what sexual practices they're willing to perform by how many Velcro straps they have on their pants. It makes me sick. Our founding fathers didn't need Velcro. They fought a revolution, against Belgium or somebody, so that they could wear their buttons. Think about it. Can you see colonial wives sewing Velcro onto their husbands' pantaloons? Their pants wouldn't have stayed up and we would've lost the revolution. We'd all be speaking Belgianese. I know. I know. But, this is America people. Take to the streets and let your leaders know that we don't want government—funded Velcro clothes. We want freedom. (dramatic pause) We want buttons."

Soon the reverberations could be felt from Alaska to Maine. People accepted O'Looney's clarion call and took to the streets, proudly wearing their buttons in politically incorrect defiance of current trends. But, the slogans didn't have as much oomph as those of other movements in the past:

"Hey, hey, government guys, how many Velcro straps have you put on our pants today?"

"No interlocking connective straps without representation!"

"1-2-3-4, let us keep our buttons and stop putting Velcro on our damn clothes you worthless, socialist, power-mongers."

"Hitler would've worn Velcro, if he'd, you know, been alive when they invented it."

And those were only the ones that kind of made sense.

Ah, the early days of The Buttonites were glorious. They banded together, grass-roots style. They circulated petitions. They successfully got Velcro banned from the state of Texas, but that was only after a compromise (first Texas threatened to secede from the Union, and, after realizing that nobody cared, they threatened to take Willie Nelson with them, so a compromise was quickly reached). Texas governor, Arnold Hamilton III, flushed with victory, lent voice to the country's concerns:

"Look, I don't hate Velcro. If they want to wear it in San Francisco, that's fine. We just don't like it down here. The federal government wants to put a hurtin' on the giant belt buckle industry, because they're clearly in the pockets of the Velcro industry."

And thus a movement was born.

TUESDAY'S THERAPY SESSION

"A pen light? A freaking pen light, that's your object? Well, you clearly lose. I don't even need to hear the rest."

Dr. Bob looked dejected. He'd really thought that the pen light would be more impressive, but Dr. Maria put him in his rightful place. Then Dr. Phil (no relation to the fat loser who sells weight loss books) chimed in:

"That's pathetic, Bob. I once found two, count 'em two copies of *US NEWS AND WORLD REPORT.* Guy said that his colon wanted to know what the deal was with the Sudan."

"Yep, that's today's winner for the weirdest thing we've found lodged in a man's anus. Once again the prize goes to Dr. Phil. He's today's biggest ass."

It was just the usual pre-meeting banter of the institutionalized proctologists' therapy group. They meet on Tuesday in their specialty asylum for professionals who went bat-shit. Doctors, as a rule, are ridiculously boring people, but certain specialties are exceptions to that rule. And the head shrink, after noticing that he had a decent number of proctologists, started an intra-medical specialty therapy group.

Dr. Jonathan Riordan (former medical supply salesman, MD, phD, and a few other d's) entered the room. He's the shrink, the doctor to these doctors.

"Hi Doctor Jonathan," they all shouted in unison.

Dr. Riordan—"You know I hate that. Call me Doctor Riordan. You guys are doctors. Didn't you ever at least try to get your patients to show you the respect of not calling you a cartoon character name?"

Dr. Maria—"Come on doc, we've been over this. People want their proctologist to have a sense of humor. And they look at us as half-clown anyway."

Dr. Bob—"Trust me, it helps. And if we don't get last names, then face it, amigo, you don't either."

Dr. Riordan—"OK, whatever. Anyway, if I remember correctly, last time we left off with Maria telling us about what led up to her freak-out. So we'll start with Maria after the chant."

Everybody—"WE'RE GOOD PEOPLE, WHO'VE DEDICATED OURSELVES TO A NOBLE CRAFT. IT'S NOT OUR FAULT THAT PEOPLE MAKE FUN OF US . . . THEY'RE JUST ASSHOLES."

And they all laughed.

Dr. Riordan—"Come on guys, you know I hate it when you ad-lib."

Dr. Phil—"If you can't laugh about this, doc, then I worry about you."

Dr. Riordan—"Anyway, Maria, when we left off last week, you were telling the group about the specific events that led you to your present circumstances."

Dr. Maria—"Yeah, well, like I said before, this woman, let's call her Phyllis, came in complaining about loose stool and rectal pain."

The group paused waiting for Dr. Bob's regular musical refrain, set to Prince's classic eighties hit, "Purple Rain", which never came.

Dr. Riordan—"Good Bob, you're laying off the jokes. That's progress."

Dr. Bob—"Oh crap, did she say rectal pain? I'll get it next time."

Dr. Riordan—"I think you missed the point, Bob. Maria, please continue."

Dr. Maria—"So, Phyllis came in complaining about, uh, about what I said before. And after the x-ray, we determined that it was a pocket watch, a nice one too, gold, inscribed. Her husband was right there beside her, comforting her. It was a nice little family scene and all, considering. Then, the next day we did the removal surgery. Again, the husband was there, holding his wife's trembling hand, saying soothing words, at least until the sedative kicked in. But once we'd retracted the watch, he must've recognized it since he couldn't take his eyes off it. Most people, you know, look the other way. It turns out that it was his brother's watch. And he'd given his brother the watch for a wedding present. And the inscription read, 'I'll always have your back.' Anyway, the brothers got into a brawl. I got sued by the wife for breaking doctor/patient confidentiality and I got written up for a HIPPA violation. That's when I lost it and started the shame spiral that landed me here with you good folks."

Dr. Bob—"His brother's watch. What are the odds?"

Dr. Maria—"You should've seen Phyllis' face when I came in with the good news/bad news situation."

Dr. Phil—"I bet. Good news, you can now defecate in peace. Bad news, you might should've kept it up in there."

Dr. Riordan—"Excellent, Maria. See folks, Maria has pinpointed the moment when her life started coming unraveled. This is progress, Maria. Thanks for sharing. Who's next today? I see Kelly is absent today, so Phil, why don't you take over."

Dr. Phil—"Yeah, well, I guess I'm the old-timer here. I told this to the last group, but Dr. J over there says that it's healthy to repeat the thing. So, I had a two-man tandem come in one day. They were pretty experimental gay lovers. You guys know what Chinese finger-cuffs are? Well, think about that, but with forearms, up to the elbow. Two of their friends had to almost roll them in. They were like the infinity symbol only more disgusting. I could spell it out, but I think this group gets the picture. Of course they gave me the standard bullshit spiel. You see doc, we're acrobats and our dream is to work for the Cirque de Soliel. I never felt the need to call the patients on the lies and this one was at least creative. So I was all set to do the surgery, but this was a two-man thing and I was a little worried about being sued. So, I made the humongous mistake of asking some of my fellow doctors for help . . . non-procties."

Drs. Maria and Bob—"Ooooohhh."

Dr. Phil—"Yeah, yeah. Well, you all know what happened next. Gossip at a hospital . . . it's like a damn sorority house . . . it travels fast. And at first the teasing was simple, regular stuff. I've got thick skin. I was used to it and non-procties aren't the most creative bunch. But they just wouldn't let it go. And then they started telling the residents and interns. Getting made fun of by newbies, I just couldn't take it. I hadn't planned on assaulting that med student, and I really hadn't planned on demonstrating the operation on him, and I reeeaaaalllly hadn't planned on using the stirrups, but I just wasn't thinking, Dr. Jon. It all went red. I don't know. It's all kind of a haze. I do regret it though . . . mostly."

Dr. Riordan—"There you go, Dr. Phil. Thank you for sharing. Good work. It looks like we're all out of time for today. We'll get to Dr. Bob's diamond smuggling story next time. Nice job today. We've got brownies over on the table."

PERVERT ISLAND

Once again, the people had gotten scared and fed up, really scared and really fed up (the people seem to get fed up a lot). Every night the news told them of yet another sexual predator who had performed some unnatural act on some unsuspecting child. That could've been their kid. At first, the people and the opportunistic politicians who "represented" them decided that it would be best if sexual offenders registered with their local police precincts. Then the police would inform the neighborhood that a pervert was about to move in next to them. This was bad for property values and blood pressure.

Then the people demanded that sex offenders wear a giant P pinned on their clothes so that parents could be sure that they were throwing garbage at the right person. But even that wasn't enough. Then Congressman Fred "Family Man" Spelman, the distinguished gentleman from Ohio, had a revelation. It was a far-reaching proposal and a complicated idea, but it captured the public's imagination like few other bills have. Thanks to the overwhelmingly popular response, Spelman knew he was onto something when he introduced the world to:

PERVERT ISLAND.

At first the people wanted to cordon off Vermont and give it to the perverts, but then where would we get our syrup? We didn't want pervert syrup. Plus, there's a lot more land in Vermont than the maps would lead you to believe and the pervert comfort level wasn't all that important to the public.

That's when Spelman decided to change his bill in committee. There was a little island in northern Ohio called Conch Shell Island, known as such for its conspicuous lack of conch shells. It had been uninhabited, as far as anyone knew, for years. The terrain was rugged and not conducive to agriculture, but perfect for molesting young people. After the bill passed almost unanimously and the proposal was given the ironic blessing of both the Family Decency Council and the North American Man/Boy Love Association, it was law.

HR2353, otherwise known as the Pervert Relocation Act, basically said just what you'd think it'd say. Once the perverts get out of jail, we round 'em up and ship 'em to the island. That way they and we can live in peace. We can let our kids walk to school, and they can have a place where they can molest each other with impunity. We can have peace of mind, and they can live free of shame and degradation. We can focus on other issues, and once a year we'll catapult truant kids over the wall and let them fight it out (the NAMBLA lobbyist got this one as a last minute concession). Overall, the country was satisfied and the ACLU decided to let this one pass.

Unbeknownst to the United States government, two older Canadian couples, fleeing a Celine Dion concert, had recently snuck over the border and made Conch Shell Island their home. They built small, cottage-like homes deep in the middle of the island. Desiring to live like hobbits in their final years, the Dirksons and the LeMonts built small dwellings which wouldn't be visible to helicopters or satellites or people or conch shells. Sam and Mary Dirkson were both satisfied to live out their golden years reading, gardening and hiding from their children. Renda and Uriah LeMont owed enough money to the Canadian government for Canada to finally, if they were to get it, achieve its dream of buying The North Pole. The two families had been living on the newly minted Pervert Island for two years when the perverts started showing up.

One day Uriah and Sam were sitting on carved rocking chairs on the LeMont front porch.

Uriah—"Sure are a lot more people here nowadays."

Sam—"Yep . . . and a surprising number of them are perverts."

The first batch of émigrés to the island had thirty seven perverts and one guy, Sam Johnson, who was actually an arsonist, but the paperwork got mixed up. Sam Johnson was scared. He'd managed to keep his rectum untouched through five years of federal prison, but this was going to be tough. Still, Sam was not a man to give up easily. When his mother said that he shouldn't burn down the 4-H Club, he took that as a challenge. When his parole officer said not to set fire to any more Mattel display racks, he disagreed. If Sam Johnson could escape unscathed from a burning roadside fireworks stand which he'd just set on fire, then he could do anything.

At first, the perverts just stood around, wondering what to do. Then, when the Air Force plane started dropping bags of canned goods, they scattered. After the memorial service for the two guys who were hit with bags of cabbage was over, they set to work creating a sexually dysfunctional utopia. Daniel "You Want some Ice Cream, Little Boy?" Velasquez was a born leader. His parents told him that he'd be president one day. That was the day before they caught him molesting the family guinea pig. Daniel suggested that they form committees. All the perverts agreed. First they needed a housing committee. Wendell "It's OK, I'm Your Uncle" Pendergrass was put in charge of the housing committee. He and five other perverts set to work gathering wood and scouting locations for houses. Next Daniel proposed that they needed a Food Committee. Greg "I Dress Up As Santa All Year Round" Henderson was put in charge of sorting the canned goods, fashioning a can opener out of twigs and berries and scouting the island for animals and edible plants. They also formed a Boy Scout committee with Zane "Strangers Have The Best Candy" Kendrick as its head. The Boy Scout committee was less about being prepared as it was about scouting for boys.

Back on the front porch:
Uriah—"Saw the new arrivals today."
Sam—"Yep. Me too. Looked kinda sketchy."
Uriah—"That's 'cause they're all perverts. Every last one. I asked."
Sam—"Americans?"
Uriah—"Of course."

The beginning of any new society, especially a revolutionary one, is always a difficult time. There's an adjustment period for anything new, and it's usually awkward. The salad days of Pervert Island were no exception. There were fights. There were angry disputes taken before the newly formed Council of Boytopia. There were property issues to be decided. And there were circle jerks. Daniel Velasquez was elected the first Prime Minister and Myron "Kinderstalker" Timonsin was elected sheriff. At first the happy perverts decided that, though some governmental structure was needed, a minimalist approach would suit them best.

After three months of confusion, progress and sexual frustration, Pervert Island was up and running. That's when FBI officer, Jennifer Halfkind, made her first surprise inspection. After repeatedly turning down her boss' sexual advances, she was assigned the unfortunate task of being the first American Ambassador to Pervert Island. Wisely, she bought a house boat with company funds and christened it the USS Embassy. Since she was the only person for thousands of miles who had a key to the fence that surrounded the island, she felt relatively safe in the embassy. She still slept with her sidearm under her pillow, but that was as much out of habit as it was due to her current geography.

"As Prime Minister, I call this first meeting of Boytopia to order."

"Here, here."

"Yes, here. Where else would it be? First order of business, progress reports. First, housing. Wendell?"

"OK. Housing. Well we've begun gathering material for building houses. In the meantime, the feds dropped off some tents, so we can stay in those until we build. I've got two guys out chopping wood and a third out with them to keep them on track and not let them molest each other."

"What if the third guy joins in the molesting?"

"Oh crap. I didn't think about that. I'll be back."

"All right. Next order of business, food. Greg?"

"OK. We've sorted all the canned goods. They dropped us a few bows and quivers of arrows, I guess for hunting. I suggest that we give the weapons to the sheriff, Myron, for safe keeping and see who can hunt."

"That's a great idea, Greg. Who can hunt?"

Steve "Let's Play A New Game" Babbit raised his hand. Known far-and-wide as The Montana Molester, Steve had a lot of experience roughing it, no pun intended. He was in one of those separatist, anti-government groups, so popular with bored upper Mid-Westerners, until they'd discovered that he was, well, you know.

"Great, Steve. You're in charge of hunting. Ask around and see if anyone else has any skills at kidnapping small defenseless creatures."

They all had a good laugh at that one. That Daniel, he is one clever pervert.

"But seriously folks, back to business. Our final committee is the Boy Scout committee. Zane?"

"I've looked. Ain't a boy in sight. This is bad."

"I know, but remember, the good people at NAMBLA negotiated us a boyapult once a year and their lobbyist told me that the first batch is coming next week. I don't know which day, but I'll set up a revolving post to monitor the area."

"Nice work, Zane. Finally, the FBI rep is staying on a house boat just outside of the gate. She's going to be coming into camp tomorrow at dinner time. I thought that it'd be nice if we had a meal laid out for her and Zane, if you do find any boys before them, be sure to hide them. Any more new business?"

"Anybody bring any Vaseline?"

"OK, meeting adjourned."

And thus began the long and storied history of Pervert Island.

MOM AND I HAVE AN AFTERNOON TOGETHER

Yeah, I know all teenage boys have a weird relationship with their mothers. We still love our mommies, but hey, we've just discovered that there are other girls out there. And, while they might not love us quite as much as our moms and they definitely don't pay for stuff like mom, they are sexier. At least it's better than teenage girls and their mothers with that constant under-the-surface love/hate Girl World crap. But still, the teenage years are a strange adjustment period for the mother/son relationship. And once you and your mother are abducted by aliens, trust me, it only gets weirder.

My mother and I were out on a Saturday afternoon, at the mall, shopping for Christmas presents, enjoying the epicenter of modern small town life, and checking out the mall rats, speed-walkers, and potential rapists who make up the extended shopping mall family.

From reading tabloids, I'd just assumed that aliens only abduct drunk rednecks when they're passed out in cornfields, but it turns out that aliens actually own the national houseware chain, The Pottery Barn. And if you accidentally take a left after the 500—thread-count bed sheet section and turn left into the stockroom, then it's a teleportation portal directly to the mother ship.

"Come on mom, it's not even all that expensive, I swear."

"Peter, it's one hundred and fifty dollars. I'm not spending that on a video game."

"But it's educational."

"*Deathmonger IV: Now We Kill The Children* is educational?"

"Sure, it teaches you about killing children."

"Funny, Peter. No, no, it's this way."

And those were the words that I heard as mom opened the swinging door and the two of us were pushed through what I can only describe as a lot like Star Trek beamer-upper-thing. As we were en route you could kind of see her words and feel them too, if that makes any sense to you . . . because it sure didn't to me.

The next thing I know my mother and I are stuck in the standing position, arms out, crucifixion style, in what looks like a round, almost empty, room. Besides the two of us, there was another mother/child combo, but this child was a girl, an attractive girl at that. She had long straight brown hair, a button nose and a wide, toothy smile, which would've been cute if her mouth hadn't been frozen in the Botoxesque super smile position. There was also a little space heater (apparently the alien has a sense of humor), next to me in the round room. After what might've been two seconds or maybe two days, we all felt the invisible restraints shut off and were free to move about the room. Both mothers instinctively hugged their children tight for a second before taking stock of the situation.

"So does this mean I'm not getting the video game, mom?"

"Hey, I'm Ethel Robinson"—my mom

"Um hi, Susan Tiggs. This is Kelly."

"Oh that's Peter."

It was the same get-to-know-you, nervous, mindless chatter that we'd employ in a doctor's waiting room (a pretty good analogy if you think about it).

"So, are we . . . ?"

"Do you think?"

"Hell yeah, mom. We've just been abducted by aliens."

"I knew we should've gone to Target."

I suppose that we were being watched, or somehow monitored, since the alien or aliens let us talk and hang out for what had to be a half an hour, but that's hard to gauge since time seems different in space. Plus, in The Pottery Barn in general, time has no meaning. But, eventually, the four of us, in the blink of an eye, were back in our former positions, up against the wall and unable to move.

That's when we first saw the alien. He wasn't green. Damn you TV. He was sort of a khaki-grey color and looked humanoid, with arms, legs, a torso, a head, two mouths and four noses, not too scary, and not all that comic booky. Luckily, he spoke perfect terse English. Being Americans, we were fortunate that he wasn't a French—speaking alien.

"Welcome to my vessel. I am sorry to have taken you. My name is Bro. Do you have any questions?"

This is one polite alien.

My mom—"Um, Bro. What do you want with us?"

"I am only here to study you, Mrs. Robinson. I have no hostile intentions."

Call me crazy or American teenage-boy homophobic, but I consider anal probing a mildly hostile intention.

And as if it weren't bad enough simply being anally probed by an alien, I just hit the teenage boy embarrassment trifecta:

Place—I'm going to be probed.

Show—It's going to be in front of my mother.

Win—And it's going to be in front of a cute girl.

I think Bro might've been a little sadistopathic, since, immediately after that thought, I was immediately transported from the wall to a medical table which itself just appeared in the middle of the room. And, naturally, I was lying on my stomach.

As Bro was sticking random objects into my colon, my mother offered advice:

"Don't fidget, Peter."

She just can't help herself.

And when Kelly was being probed and I was trying to be encouraging/hitting on her mercilessly, my mom couldn't hide her disapproval.

"Look at how she's dressed, Peter." Lowering her voice, "She's a slut."

Of course Kelly's mom heard this. The acoustics are amphitheater-like here in space.

"Are you calling my daughter a slut?"

"She's not good enough for my Peter."

"Mom, come on . . . at least wait until they're done rectally probing her?"

If I thought being interspecies molested in front of my mom was embarrassing, even that couldn't compare with watching my mom get probed. But I guess Bro sensed my impending fear and the three of us, sans my mom, were sent back down to Pottery Barn as soon as my mom hit the table. Mom appeared back on Earth a minute later.

Now, in this, hopefully, unique, situation, what do you say to your fellow captees?

—Give me your email address, I'll write

—Let's go to the cops/TV News/National Enquirer

—Y'all want to check out the throw pillows
—Holy Shit, did that just really happen?

Those are pretty much the only options.

We chose the third.